REFUGE OF THE DEAD

JEREMY DYSON

DARTMOOR
PUBLISHING

REFUGE OF THE DEAD
Book Four in the Realm of the Dead Series
Copyright © 2020 by Jeremy Dyson
DARTMOOR BOOKS
Cover Design by Jeremy Dyson

ISBN: 9780990398479

For Ben

PROLOGUE

I saw her abandoned car. The blood. Her broken cell phone. Hundreds of dead bodies. I was so sure Amanda was gone forever.

But my wife is alive.

Even as I stand here looking at her, I'm afraid to let myself believe it.

"Blake," she says. Her voice is soft and hoarse and barely more than a whisper.

My legs move, carrying me closer to her. I reach out and place my hands lightly on her shoulders. It feels like if I touch her she might just vanish again. All of this is so surreal. My hands hang on to her frail body as if she might slip away again should I let go of her.

So I don't.

I wrap my arms around her and pull her close to me.

Her parched lips curl into a grimace and she begins to cry.

Her current condition is heartbreaking. The neglected, greasy hair smells of smoke. The torn and stained clothes that she wears reek of stale sweat. Her face is gaunt and covered with grime. None of that causes me any hesitation as I kiss her on the forehead.

"I thought you were gone," I whisper as she cries into my chest.

Her fingers clench the fabric of my shirt and she clings to me tightly as she continues to sob.

I am overcome with guilt. My wife was alive all this time. Though I realize the odds of ever finding her, even if I had not given up, were astronomical, I still feel a sharp stab of regret that I did not do more. I should have never assumed anything. But after finding my daughter like I did... I lost hope. I had no choice but force myself to accept that my old life was gone in order to move on.

"I'm sorry," I whisper to her, over and over again. "I'm so sorry."

Everything else is momentarily forgotten.

The fact that Chase had gone out this morning without me when he knew damn well I was coming. The fact that Danielle is standing right there behind me, watching us. None of that matters right now.

I clutch Amanda in my arms, still not able to believe she is really there. It had taken months for me to even begin to come to terms with losing everything and everyone that mattered to me. Finally, I had to accept that truth and tried to move on with my life.

But everything is not gone. I was wrong.

Apologies keep coming from my lips as I release my wife and look at her, but she just stares without expression at the buttons of my shirt. Something feels so off about her. She seems hollow and even afraid of me for some reason. I search her eyes for some sign of the woman I remember, but something seems so different. I place my hand on her shoulder and she retracts from my touch.

She must have endured so much outside. It will take time. Of course. She will need some time.

I try to smile again, but Amanda will not even look me in the eyes. Her head tilts forward and she stares down at the floor.

Even though it still seems like I'm holding on to the ghost of the woman I married, the sight of her face fills me with hope. I thought I'd lost everything, but I was wrong all along.

If I can find her again, maybe it means we can try to piece our broken world back together. There might still be hope for all of us. We can still be the people we were before all this. It might take a while to get there, but one day things might be like they used to be again.

CHAPTER ONE

My brooding eyes stare at the empty shelf before me until the sudden crash of shattering glass startles me. Ringing bits of the bottle rain down to the tile floor. I abandon the empty shelves in front of me and I glance over my shoulder to see Hawk grab another empty liquor bottle off the counter of the pharmacy and launch it against the shelves along the wall. It crashes against the metal rack and more shards rain down to the floor.

"Hawkins, would you mind knocking that shit off?" Chase warns him. "Don't need to let the whole fucking world know we're in here."

"I'm just getting so fucking sick of this," Hawkins complains. "We're out here busting our asses every day, and for what?"

Hawkins lofts another bottle at the wall. Chase clenches his jaw and shoots him an irritated stare before he returns his focus to searching the shelves.

Stitch leans his scruffy body against me and lets out a sound that is something between a pathetic snarl and a whimpering groan. I glance down and see his one good ear perked up and listening as he looks around for the source of the sound. The other ear flops to the side in the usual fashion. The mutt senses me staring down at him and looks up at me. He wags his tail and opens his mouth and pants heavily. I'm not really sure if he was trying to protect me or hide behind me.

"Stupid dog," I mutter.

Stitch trots off and resumes sniffing around the floor near the entrance to the store.

"This is a fucking waste of time," says Hawk.

He shakes his head, takes out a towel from his pack, and wipes the layer of sweat off his scalp of blonde stubble. It's been a long hot summer, and it's not over yet. Even though it's almost September, it still feels as if this summer, like the dead, just refuses to die.

"Reapers have picked this whole damn town clean," Natalie agrees.

"Same as everywhere," adds Scout as she pushes aside a collection of empty allergy medicine packages only to find the desolate shelf behind them.

"This is pointless," Lana says.

"I second that," Hawkins agrees.

Staff Sergeant Matthew Hawkins and Officer Lana Gomez are the last two members sent from Cheyenne Mountain to accompany our team. Initially, there were about a dozen volunteers, but these two are the only ones left that are still alive.

Even though most of the personnel inside Cheyenne Mountain served in the Air Force, the vast majority of them primarily handled administrative or technical aspects. Their tactical experience and training are minimal. They are great if you need a satellite image of a location or want to launch a missile strike, but not so experienced with close-quarters combat.

The Chair Force. That's what Chase calls them. They don't appreciate it too much, but I have to admit it is pretty accurate.

They've been locked inside since the beginning. Most of them prefer to keep it that way for as long as possible.

I can't really say I blame them.

It must be easier to watch it all happen on the screen of a monitor. You can imagine it is something that doesn't impact you... pretend you aren't a part it at all.

If I'm being honest, I wish I could have done that, too. It's a hell of lot easier.

Once you've witnessed this kind of horror, you can never forget it, though. I can't sit inside and act like they do. Like everything is normal. I've tried. The nightmare is all that feels real anymore.

Most of the volunteers that we had initially came from

the site security unit. Prior to this, their biggest job was check name badges or guard entrances, but they were mostly young and, at the very least, their roles required them to use a rifle on a regular basis.

Well, carry a rifle.

Still, the security teams weren't prepared for the kind of situations we encountered out there. After a pair of conflicts with the Reapers in which we sustained some heavy losses, no one volunteered to leave the base anymore.

Chase says it was for the best. Too many people out there just increases the odds that someone will fuck up. Statistically speaking, he might be on to something.

Aside from the military personnel, the rest of the people that reside inside the bunker are either scientists that worked for NASA or part of the site support staff. Janitors, cooks, and medical staff. That sort of thing.

Except for Lana.

Officer Lana Gomez was a Colorado Springs police officer. She helped the secret service to escort Senator McGrath to Cheyenne Mountain when this whole nightmare began. McGrath is the man that eventually became the new president of our devastated country. All thanks to Lana. If it hadn't been for her and her partner that died, we wouldn't have a president at all.

So here we are. Together, our six-person team is tasked with scavenging essential supplies so that perhaps Claire and Doctor Schoenheim can still find a way to save us all.

The Cheyenne Mountain Complex has a lot of facilities, but it's still not that same as a laboratory. We also have to acquire a supply of Donepezil for the doctor. It's a dementia medication. Without it, he can hardly remember to put on his pants let alone do his research.

It's hard to believe that the fate of humanity may hinge on our success or failure, but that seems to be the reality of it. That thought is what keeps us going on days like this when luck is not on our side. We don't have much of a choice.

I make eye contact with Scout and she lets out a frustrated sigh and shakes her head to tell me that she has not found anything of use here either.

"What time is it, Nat?" Chase wonders.

Natalie stretches her arm to reveal the wristwatch beneath her sleeve. Her eyes glance down at the numbers and then she shrugs the sleeve back into place.

"Almost o-fifteen hundred," Natalie tells him as she readjusts her grip on the rifle.

Ever since we met Chase, Natalie has emulated him as much as possible. Her attitude changed completely in the last month, and I can't say for sure that it is an improvement. Maybe she thinks if she can be hard and cold enough that nothing will get to her anymore.

But I'm not so sure.

There is only so long a person can avoid dealing with things before it becomes too much to handle.

"Let's move out," Chase says. "We can still make it to the next town and get back to base before dark."

"What's the point?" Hawk sighs. "We been out here for days and what do we have to show for it? Nothing."

If I hadn't known Hawkins for a couple of weeks now, some of his complaints might make me think he is just a jaded asshole. Except I know the reason for it. He used to be a pretty nice guy, but his attitude changed after he watched every soldier under his command die brutally at the hands of the undead. That kind of thing is bound to weigh on a man, no matter if he is as tough as Hawkins or not.

"We can't give up," I say. "Not if we want to survive."

Stitch lets out a whimper and then a low growl as he stares out the windows at the front of the store. I turn my head to see him watching the street through the cloudy glass.

Must be corpses.

Scout walks by me while I grab up my pack and rifle from the floor and get ready to move.

"How many?" Chase asks Scout as she swipes a hand to clear the glass and peeks outside.

"Just a couple so far," Scout says as she pushes open the door at the front of the pharmacy and turns her head to check up and down the block. She turns and looks back into the dark interior of the store and jerks her head toward the street.

"Come on," she urges us. "Let's get the hell out of here while it's still somewhat clear."

We follow her outside toward the pair of bullet-riddled black Tahoes. Nearby corpses trudge toward us through the overgrown grasses and wildflowers that surround the small parking lot. Rotting grey flesh clings to their vacant faces. Their moans are now hoarse and raspy, a symptom of the decomposition of their vocal cords over the last several months.

Stitch runs out to the middle of the road and bares his teeth and snarls at the corpses as they approach us.

"Come on, you idiot," I call to the dog. After a corpse lunges at him, Stitch stops acting tougher than he is and lets out a high-pitched yelp before he retreats to the vehicle. He jumps into the backseat with Lana and squeezes by her legs to get to the other side of the seat while she slams the door.

Natalie raises her rifle and fires a carefully aimed shot. One of the corpses falls to the dirt.

"Don't waste the bullets," I remind her. "They're not close enough to be a threat to us."

Natalie lowers the rifle slightly and squints her eyes at me as I climb behind the wheel of the second vehicle.

"She needs the practice anyway," Chase disagrees. He gives her a slight nod and she raises the rifle back up and aims at the other walking corpse and fires. The head of the things snaps back, its legs buckle, and it collapses. Its head smacks against the pavement and spills putrid brain matter onto the pavement.

"That a girl," Chase says. "Good shot."

He glances back at me once more before he slides behind the wheel of the lead vehicle and fires up the engine.

I let out a sigh as Scout climbs into the passenger seat beside me. She can probably tell I'm frustrated, but she just pulls the aviator sunglasses off the collar of her shirt and puts them on. She just wants to stay out of it. Can't really say I blame her for that.

After Stevie lost his father, no one thought Scout would consider coming out with us and leaving him behind. I guess she realizes we aren't finished yet. This isn't the kind of world she wants to leave for the kid.

But it's not so easy for her to leave him behind either. Every minute she is away from him out here it visibly weighs on her.

Once everyone is in both vehicles, I turn the key and crank the ignition. I wait a few seconds until the lead vehicle begins to move and then I shift the engine into drive and follow Chase as he leads us out of town.

"He just has to disagree with everything I say," I mumble.

I hadn't realized I was talking out loud until after I said it, but everyone in the car ignores me anyway. They know how I had nearly pulled the trigger and shot Chase. Some days I still wonder if I should have. I wanted to, but I was afraid of the kind of person that would make me.

Things like that don't just go away. They're like infected wounds that fester just beneath the surface of the skin. Eventually, they might kill you unless you deal with them. After I let out another frustrated sigh, I try my best to forget it for now.

This isn't the time or the place.

Our convoy zigs and zags through the abandoned cars along the mountain roads. The late August sun hangs in the distance in cloudless Colorado sky and the heat waves emanating from the blacktop melt the hazy horizon.

A massive bug splatters against the windshield, leaving another starburst of slime across the filthy glass. I try the wipers but the washer fluid tank is bone dry and the blade smears the insect guts.

Figures.

Lately, it seems like trying to fix anything is a surefire way to make the problem worse.

"That's great," I sigh and shut the wipers off.

The brake lights ahead of us glow red. Chase slows the lead vehicle down when we approach the next community. The tires crunch through broken glass on the ground as we squeeze the pair of trucks between two smashed vehicles. As soon as we emerge from the wreck, a pair of ragged corpses moan and toss their bodies against my door. I recoil from the hideous faces crashing against the glass and chomping their teeth.

"Shit," I curse. But I resist the urge to stomp on the gas. Instead, I ease the pedal down and pull away from them. I watch the things stumbling along behind us for a moment then focus on the road ahead of me once again.

The sight of the dead is welcome these days. At least we know this town might not have been cleaned out already. We may even salvage what we need.

We can only hope.

That's the only thing that keeps us going these days.

CHAPTER TWO

The bodies of the dead run into the road and throw themselves against the lead vehicle. They bounce off and collapse on the pavement, right in my path. I swerve to try and avoid the disfigured bodies and am mostly successful.

Chase skids to a stop on the dusty road in the center of town. Behind him, I slam the brakes as well.

Corpses shamble toward our vehicles. Some of the recently departed show only slight decomposition, while several others are in such bad shape they crawl along the ground. Fresh or not, the dead are all still extremely dangerous, though. Anyone that forgets that, even for a moment, does not have long to live.

Rifle barrels appear out of the rear windows of the Tahoe in front of us and begin firing on anything that gets too close. Scout rolls down the window beside me and takes aim with her pistol. She opens fire as well.

My hand reaches down and finds the assault rifle nestled between my leg and the center console. I push open the door and take a quick look around. We have maybe ten or fifteen stiffs still coming at us from different directions. Nothing we can't handle. We have countless times before. But you never know when things might go wrong.

My finger squeezes the trigger after I take aim at a guy in tattered jeans and a green trucker hat. The first shot hits him in the neck and he stumbles closer, but I pull the trigger again and the round knocks his head back.

He collapses on the asphalt close enough that I catch the acrid scent of rotting meat. The smell fills my nostrils. I do my best to ignore it while I turn to locate another target.

A hunter in an orange vest emerges from behind a cabin and shuffles through the waist-high grass. I take aim, but hold my fire when I notice the large propane tank along the side of the building. Maybe it's empty, but if it isn't and I miss my mark, which is entirely possible, god only knows what kind of damage it might do.

I decide not to risk it. There are other targets. Some are even closer than the hunter by the tank. I lower the gun and glance around at the dead people that close in all around us.

"What the hell are you doing?" Chase yells when he pauses to reload his weapon. He shakes his head at me when I look at him. "Fucking shoot them." He slaps a fresh magazine into his assault rifle and returns his focus on the approaching threats.

I refocus my gaze back on the corpse near the propane tank. I take an extra moment to aim before I finally take the shot. The bullet tears through the skull of the thing, but my heart skips a beat when I hear a ping as the bullet ricochets off the side of the big red tank. I hold my breath for several seconds and wait for the explosion, but nothing happens.

When I realize the blast is not coming, I scan the area for more targets. Bodies, riddled with bullets, litter the area. The rest of the team has already made quick work of the dead.

"Clear," Chase yells out.

Several of the others respond to confirm that all threats are eliminated. An eerie silence returns in the aftermath. We take a look around the street at what the small town has to offer.

A rundown filling station.

A general store and a diner.

A car repair shop and a hair salon.

That's about it. It could be worse, but it could be a lot better, too.

"Let's split up into teams," Chase suggests.

"Sounds good," I agree.

"You two are with me," he looks at Natalie and Hawk

and jerks his head. "We'll take everything on the west side of the road. Thirty minutes."

I nod and return to the Lincoln to grab some empty duffel bags from the back. I follow Scout and Lana as toward the general store, scanning the area for any signs of movement. We may have cleared the dead that wandered the streets, but that does not mean it is okay to think it is safe. There is always the chance that more of those things are lingering nearby. They could be trapped inside one of the nearby buildings. There is also the chance that the sounds of gunfire might attract more of the dead that are in the surrounding area.

There is the possibility that we might run into other survivors, too. It doesn't happen very often anymore out here. Most survivors out here are hiding way up in the mountains and they don't want to be found.

Then, of course, there are the Reapers.

Metal cans crash to the floor inside the store and stop us in our tracks. We stare at the door for several seconds and listen again. I shift the straps of the duffel bags hanging from my shoulder and adjust my grip on the rifle to be ready to take out whatever the hell might be in there if it should come through the door. Out here in the sunlight, it's impossible to tell what might be lurking inside.

"You alive in there?" Scout says.

We listen for several seconds but we get no response. I

take another few steps toward the entrance of the shop, but I freeze when something else crashes inside.

"Fuck this," mutters Lana. She hoists her submachine gun up and a second later she opens fire. Bullets tear through the cracked front windows of the store and glass shatters loudly on the sidewalk. Lana keeps shooting until she runs out of bullets and smoke drifts up from the muzzle of her gun. I listen for any more sounds as she swaps in a fresh magazine, but the area seems quiet once again.

"What?" Lana says. I turn to see Scout scowling at the woman and shaking her head.

"What do you mean what?" Scout says. "We're out here risking our lives to search for this stuff only to have you shoot it all up as soon as we find it. Jesus."

"No," said Lana. "I'm not risking my life out here. Not at all. Nothing out here is worth dying for. Not anymore."

"Alright," I interrupt them to end the discussion before they end up in an argument. It happens a lot out here. Every single one of us can be a little on edge at times. "Let's just do this. We don't have much sunlight left."

I walk around Scout and step up the curb. My boots crack the pieces of the glass on the sidewalk as I make my way to the door. Another loud crash greets me as I reach for the handle. I have a look inside and spot a rotating rack of sunglasses that just toppled to the floor. My eyes scan upwards and I see the feet of a body that dangles from the rafters. The rest of the corpse comes into view as my fingers wrap around the doorknob.

The man appears to have been the pharmacist here, judging by his white jacket. As my gaze drifts up toward the ceiling I notice the length of rope tied around the rafters. I take another noisy step through the crunching shards on the floor and the man jerks at the sound. His rotted eyeballs dangle like dead grapes on the vine but I suppose he can still hear us. I slowly bring the rifle up while he kicks his feet and stretches his arms in my direction. Then I squeeze the trigger and put him to rest forever.

Poor bastard. I'm sure ending up like that was not part of his plan.

Scout and Lana are already searching through the shelves of the store, but I decide to clear the backroom just to be safe. We don't need any surprises.

"Be careful," Scout reminds me as I approach the door marked with an EMPLOYEES ONLY sign.

"I'll be fine," I say as I tap softly against the door.

Silence.

I nudge open the door and poke the barrel of the rifle through the crack and peer into the darkness. When nothing comes rushing at me, I push the door all the way open.

"It's clear," I tell them.

I pull down a large bag of dog food off a shelf beside the door and use it to prop the door open so that some light from the storefront will filter into the windowless stockroom. The dust in here makes my throat itch. Allergies or something. I feel it start to close up and have to clear it several times as I look around the aisles of shelves.

There is plenty of useful stuff here, but our cargo space in the Tahoe is pretty small. We can't bring back anything that isn't essential.

Food. Water. Medicine. Ammunition.

Those are still the top priorities.

Clothes, tools, and any equipment and supplies for the research lab are also vital to our longterm survival.

Even though the bunker at Cheyenne Mountain was stocked with plenty of supplies, it was not meant to sustain this many people indefinitely. The fuel that powers the facility will run out within a few months unless we find more or find a way to get the local power restored, but that is a long shot, to say the least. Still, the fact that we have even started to discuss trying to turn the local power back on as an eventual possibility seems to be a good sign for the future.

I turn on the flashlight attached to the rifle to get some extra light and aim the beam at the boxes stacked against the wall to read the labels. There is plenty of dry goods to pick from. I shoulder the rifle and grab one of the boxes full of cans of soup and make my way back to the car. After I pop open the trunk and set the heavy box in the back, Chase and his team emerge from the shop across the street empty-handed.

"Find anything good?" Chase asks me.

"Yeah," I say. "Still got to check out the pharmacy, but there's plenty inside. More than we have room for."

"That's a good problem to have for once," Chase flashes a rare smile. "We'll load up as much as we can and come back for the rest tomorrow."

"It's about time we got lucky," Natalie agrees.

"It's all about perseverance," Chase says. "Luck had nothing to do with it."

I leave the trunk open and follow the others back toward the entrance of the general store. Then I hear a distant rattle of gunfire to the north. We pause in front of the store and look up the road toward the opposite end of town.

"How far away was that?" Natalie asks.

"Not far," Hawk says.

More gunshots ring out. These aren't handguns either. It sounds like multiple assault weapons being fired on full auto.

Reapers.

"We better hurry," I say.

We all dash back inside the general store and start grabbing as much as we can and filling the duffel bags.

"Two minutes!" Chase warns us as he grabs boxes of cough medicine and bandages off the shelf and shoves them in a bag. "Grab whatever you can and let's get the fuck out of here."

I hop over the counter and start to look on the shelves

of the pharmacy. My eyes scan the hundreds of labels looking for Donepezil.

"The gunshots are getting closer!" Natalie says.

"Let's move!" I hear Chase yell.

I give up and just start grabbing everything in sight and shoving it in the duffel bag. I just have to hope that one of the medications will be something the doctor can use. If not, Doctor Schoenheim isn't going to be able to take care of himself, let alone save the rest of us from the undead.

As soon as the bag is full, I zip it close and run for the vehicles. Everyone else has already left the building. Even though we cleared the street several minutes before, more corpses are already stumbling into the road surrounding the store. The growls of the engines grow louder as the vehicles approach the edge of town.

"Reapers," Scout says. "Lots of them." She pulls her eye away from the scope and lowers her rifle. After she tosses her pack inside, Scout hops into the passenger seat of the Tahoe.

Chase tosses a duffel bag in the back. He grits his teeth and stares up the road for a few seconds. He isn't the kind of guy that would run from a fight, even when he knows the odds are against him. But he isn't stupid. Even he realizes we don't stand a chance.

"Go! Go! Go!" Chase urges us to move faster.

I take a moment to glance down the road while I hop into my seat. A small convoy of armored vehicles speeds toward us.

Narco tanks.

The Reapers created these moving fortresses by fitting various types of vehicles with thick steel plates, turrets, murder holes, and insulating the interior with a layer of bulletproof chemical foam. The improvised fighting vehicles, or IFVs, as Chase has taken to calling them, were popular among the cartel in Mexico and South America. Some of these drug lords were locked up in the supermax prison in Colorado known as the Alcatraz of the Rockies. It's no surprise they have used these same inventions to survive the apocalypse.

I can see at least a dozen of them kicking up a cloud of dust off the road. There could be even more concealed behind them.

Corpses converge on our vehicle just as I slam the door shut. The dead smear their rotting faces against the windows. They smudge black streaks of filth and decay on the glass.

I start the engine. The tires of the other Tahoe squeal as Chase pulls back around to retreat the way we came. He plows through several dead bodies in the way and floors the gas as the first of the Reapers reaches the edge of town.

The muzzle of the gun atop the lead narco tank flashes. A barrage of bullets hits our vehicle a moment later. One of the rounds hits the rear window. I duck instinctively when I hear the loud crack and then breathe a sigh of relief when I check the rearview mirror and see the bulletproof glass is still intact. My eyes focus back on the road as I try to weave through the bodies walking around on the street.

"They're slowing down," Lana says.

I glance back up to the mirror as we leave town and realize she is right. None of the vehicles are bothering to chase after us. Instead, the Reapers have stopped in the center of town and focus their attention on the remaining undead on the streets.

"They're after the town," I say. "Not us."

CHAPTER THREE

"Nope," Scout says. She tosses down the medicine bottle in her hands and zips the duffel bag closed again.

"Are you sure?" I ask her.

"I checked twice," she says. "No Donepezil."

"Great," I sigh.

"There might be something similar," she says. "I haven't heard of half the drugs here."

A silence fills the vehicle as we ride home in the orange glow of the sunset. Scout puts on her sunglasses and slumps down in the seat as Lana stares at the horizon.

"Maybe we'll have better luck tomorrow," Scout finally says.

I can tell by the flat tone of her voice that she does not really believe that.

"That's what we said yesterday," Lana says. "And the day before that."

With every day that goes by out here, we seem to have less and less luck scavenging anything of value. And it is just a matter of time before we will have to deal with the Reapers. We might be safe inside the fortress of Cheyenne Mountain, but everything else around here belongs to the Reapers or the dead.

"Well tomorrow could still be different," Scout says.

"Yeah," I nod in agreement with Scout. "Tomorrow."

"Eventually," Scout says. "We are going to have to fight them."

"It might not come to that," says Lana. She leans forward and pokes her head between the front seats. "They can't survive forever out here."

"Seems like they're doing okay to me," Scout says. "Every day we have to drive further and further to find someplace that they haven't looted."

"Still," says Lana as she leans back in her seat. "We can outlast them. I'm sure of it."

"As long as they don't figure out where to find us. Once they figure that out, they will come for us," Scout says. "They might already know."

"They'll never get inside," Lana says. "Cheyenne Mountain is a fortress."

"There is always a way," Scout says.

I think back to the complex in Missouri and I know Scout is right.

"You're just being paranoid," Lana waves a hand dismissively. "They didn't even bother to follow us this time."

"You haven't had to survive out here for months like the rest of us. You don't know what people will do to each other now just to survive. And these aren't just ordinary people. They're criminals. Some of the worst in the world."

As much as I know what they are talking about is important, I have a lot of my own problems on my mind.

After we made it to Cheyenne Mountain, I began to believe that we could start to build some sort of a normal life for ourselves again. Maybe we had lost everything, but we had a chance to start over.

Then I laid eyes on Amanda again. She appeared like an apparition. Suddenly, as though she appeared out of nothing, she was there. She may have looked like the woman I knew, but she bore no resemblance to her otherwise. From the moment I touched her, I could feel how little of the person I remembered was actually still there.

It's been a couple of weeks since Amanda was found by Scout and Chase while they were out scavenging for supplies. It was such a shock to discover she was still alive. Everything seems so much more complicated.

Sometimes, she still looks at me like she hardly recognizes me and if I look at her too closely, she will avert her eyes as if to try and hide whatever it is about her that she doesn't want me to see.

I know being out there will take a toll on anyone. It

nearly broke me. Maybe she just needs more time. I don't know.

It could be that we are just not the same people that we were just a few months ago.

After finding her vehicle abandoned, and then seeing our daughter turned into one of those monsters, I forced myself to accept that they were gone. I had to or the pain of losing them would have destroyed me.

Danielle was there for me. She kept me from completely falling apart. Eventually, I'd even started to put it all behind me. I wanted to find a way to move on, and together with Danielle, I finally started to look ahead to our future again.

Danielle has been more than understanding since Amanda resurfaced, but everything between us changed immediately. Even though she wants to be there for me, she has tried to put some distance between us at the same time. She took on extra shifts in the clinic when some of the staff got sick.

She wants to give me and Amanda the chance to figure things out. However, I can hardly get Amanda to talk to me at all. It seems easier to avoid talking about it altogether for now.

That was when I decided to start going back out with the others to scavenge. I figure if I keep busy enough, I don't have to deal with the problems that I have been avoiding. If we don't see each other, we don't need to talk about things or lie about the things we don't want to talk about.

"Blake," Scout says.

"Yeah?" I say.

She looks at me expecting an answer of some kind, but I have no idea what she was saying.

"Sorry, I wasn't listening," I confess.

"Jesus," Scout says. "I just asked if you're okay. You've been staring through the windshield like a damn zombie for ten minutes."

"Yeah," I say again. "Just a lot on my mind."

"I can drive if you want," she offers.

"That's alright," I say. "I'm good."

She keeps her eyes fixed on me for a few more moments, studying my expression.

"It'll get easier," she finally says. "Just give it time."

I nod and give her an appreciative smile before I turn to look at the road again.

I know Scout thinks she understands. She had been married, but still got pretty attached to Fletcher before he died. Still, it's not the same. She can't possibly understand how uncomfortable I feel all the time. I can barely wrap my head around the complexity of all of it at once too.

"We just need a little music," I say. I flip open the console and search for the album I left there but it's suddenly missing. "Damn," I sigh.

"What?" Scout says.

"Can you see if the CD fell on the floor?" I ask Scout.

"It's not on the floor," Lana says. "I threw that bullshit music in the garbage where it belongs."

"What?" I gasp.

"You heard me," Lana says.

"That was The Cure," I say.

"No it wasn't," Lana says.

Scout covers her mouth to stifle a laugh in the passenger seat.

"Don't look at me," Scout says. "I had nothing to do with it."

"You know how hard it's going to be to find that a copy of that album again?" I say.

"I think you'll live," Scout says.

"It was The Cure," I repeat.

"I did you a favor," Lana says. "That music was terrible."

"Guess we'll just enjoy some peace and quiet then," I say and shake my head.

In the rearview mirror, I notice Lana turns and silently stares out the window at the evergreens and shacks alongside the mountain road. We enter another small town where flies buzz around the dozens of bodies rotting in the street. Spray paint covers the walls of several buildings. Everything of value has been taken. This is what it looks like after the reapers have been through here.

They're like a pack of hyenas that will not stop until there is nothing left anywhere.

"They're taking everything," Scout says, as though she could hear my thoughts. "Everywhere we go is like this."

"Not everywhere," Lana says.

I know what she is about to say before she even finishes saying it.

"Forget it," I say. "It's suicide."

"So is doing nothing," Lana says.

"What is she talking about?" Scout asks.

"Denver," I say. "It's the only place that even the Reapers won't go."

"That's why we could probably find what we need there," Lana says.

"It's still too dangerous," I sigh. "We don't have the resources for that kind of massive operation."

"I don't like it any more than you do," Lana says. "But it's the only sure way to find what you're looking for."

The sentence hangs in the air for a moment. If we don't get the medication for Doctor Schoenheim and fast, there won't be anyone left to save. Deep down I know she is right, but going into a city like Denver is not the kind of risk I'd be willing to take anymore.

"We'll find another way," I finally say. "There has to be a better solution."

Scout turns her head away from me. She places her elbow on the door and rests her chin on her hand as she looks at the sunset. Sometimes I can't help feel like the sun is slowly setting on all of us each day. It's only a matter of time before it goes down forever and darkness takes over everything once and for all.

There was a brief moment where it didn't feel that way. Right after we arrived at Cheyenne Mountain, I'd felt optimistic that even though we had a lot of work to do, that we might be able to overcome the odds. But now, I'm not so sure about that. I'm just hoping we find a way to make it through the winter. It seems less and less likely each day.

Finally, as the dim twilight succumbs to the over-whelming black of night, we pull up the winding mountain road and stop in front of the heavy steel doors on the side of the mountain. Several corpses clamber at the impene-trable barrier, scratching their fingernails against the metal and moaning until our headlights shining on them draw them toward the vehicles.

Massive floodlights atop the doors turn on and bathe the entire area in light. We idle for a moment as the infected start to surround the vehicle.

An alarm sounds as the door begins to open and then both of the SGR- A1 sentry guns mounted above the entrance open fire on the corpses. These guns were designed by Samsung as a means to replace human sentries along the demilitarized zone. Now, they keep the dead from trapping us inside.

Chase and I pull the vehicles into the tunnel. As soon as we pull to a stop the doors begin to close again. The two panels slam together with a loud boom that echoes all the way down the dimly lit tunnel.

We continue toward the facility and pull up to the front entrance. After I park the Tahoe just outside of the open blast doors and cut off the engine, we climb out of the vehicles. I raise my arms and take a minute to stretch after the long car ride.

These days have been some of the longest ones I've ever had. We wake up before dawn and leave as soon as the sun rises, and then search the countryside until after nine in the evening when night falls again.

I glance over and notice Danielle waiting for me just inside the blast doors. Even though she still has on the scrubs that she wears in the clinic, Danielle looks like she just woke up. I'm willing to bet that she fell asleep with them on and didn't have enough time to change them since she woke up. But still, she made it down here with Stevie to wait for us to return.

I grab my rifle, close the door, and head to the entrance behind the rest of the team. Stitch trots along beside me and then runs when he spots Stevie up ahead.

"Welcome back," Danielle smiles once she realizes that everyone that left made it back alive. "Is everyone okay?" she asks.

"We're all fine," Scout says as she walks up and crouches down in front of Stevie. She wraps her arms around the kid and holds him. "What are you still doing up?"

"I tried to sleep," Stevie whines. "But it doesn't feel like night time."

"Come on," Scout says. "Let's get you to bed."

She stands up and leads the boy down the hall by the hand. Then she glances back over her shoulder at Danielle.

"Thanks for keeping an eye on him," Scout says. "Hope he wasn't too much trouble."

"It's no problem," Danielle smiles. "He was no trouble at all."

The kid smiles up at Scout.

"Can I get ice cream for being good?" he asks.

"You should be in bed," she says.

He stares down at his shoes and lets out a sigh.

"Okay," Scout relents. She ruffles his hair. "Come on."

They turn around and head back toward the cafeteria.

"I'm such a sucker," Scout mumbles as she walks by us again.

"Have fun," Danielle smiles and gives Stevie a thumbs up.

A hand suddenly smacks me hard on my back and catches me off guard. I jerk my head around abruptly.

"Good work out there today," Chase says to me. I can't be sure, but I'm pretty sure I hear some sarcasm in his tone. With him, it is never really easy to tell.

"Thanks," I mumble.

"Goodnight," Natalie waves.

The two of them head down the hall toward the sleeping quarters but Chase looks back over his shoulder at me and gives me a smirk.

"Everything alright?" Danielle asks me.

I shift my eyes to meet hers.

"Yeah," I say. "I guess."

She takes a step closer to me, wraps her arms around

my waist and gives me a quick hug that takes me slightly by surprise. It takes a few seconds before I place my hand gently on her back. Then she lets go just as quickly and takes a step back.

"I'm glad you're back," she says carefully, as though the wrong words might slip out if she was not cautious enough.

The awkwardness she feels is obvious. I feel it, too. Instead of trying to say something that inevitably makes the recent distance between us even more explicit, I just give her a tired smile and then we quietly head to our room where we lay apart from each other in the darkness and feel guilty and alone until we fall asleep.

CHAPTER FOUR

In the darkness, Danielle stifles a cough as she blindly feels around for her scrubs. I open my eyelids but only see the coffin black inside of our windowless room. My arm reaches for the desk beside the bed and I feel the small lamp on the table and twist the knob to turn on the light, and then I recoil from the sudden blinding glare.

Danielle lets out a sigh as she sees the scrubs hanging over the backrest of the chair and shoves them into a duffel bag.

"Sorry," she says. "I was trying not to wake you."

I glance up at the clock on the wall. It's just after four in the morning.

"Why are you up so early?" I ask her.

"I was hoping to get a workout in after breakfast," she says.

The last couple of weeks Danielle has been spending several hours a day in the gym. It started right after Amanda arrived, which may have been a coincidence, but probably is not. Her reason was that it helps when she feels cooped up inside here. Which makes sense, I guess.

"Again?" I ask her.

"What?" she says.

I decide not to elaborate.

"Hang on," I say. "I'll come down and eat breakfast with you."

"It's okay," she says. She pauses to clear her throat slightly. "You had a long day yesterday. Get some more rest."

I get the feeling that she might be wanting some time to herself. Maybe she is trying to avoid me. When I start to sit up, Stitch gets to his feet and climbs on me and begins licking at my face. I push him away from me and then he hops down on the floor.

"I'm good," I insist. I slide to the edge of the bed and grab my shirt hanging off the bedpost. "I was kind of hoping we could talk."

There is a long silence as Danielle stops packing her things.

"Okay," she finally agrees.

I throw on some clothes and then we step out into the hallway and head for the cafeteria. Danielle walks quietly beside me while I yawn and comb my fingers through my unruly hair.

We get to the empty cafeteria and grab a couple of trays just as the kitchen staff is putting the first platters of food on the buffet. I spoon some spongy scrambled eggs onto my plate alongside a pair of greasy sausage links.

Stitch watches my every move closely.

I start to head for one of the tables, but turn and grab one more sausage and toss it to Stitch. The dog recoils after it hits him in the face. Then he sees the meat on the floor and returns to inspect it.

I put my plate down across from Danielle and return to grab us each a cup of coffee. She is nearly halfway done eating by the time I get back to the table and sit down.

"Thanks," she says when I set the coffee down beside her plate.

"Of course," I bend down to give her a kiss on the cheek just as her hand holding the fork carries the food to her lips. She flinches suddenly and the food spills on her lap.

"Shoot," she says. She removes the food from her lap and places it on the tray beside her plate.

"Sorry," I say and move back to the other side of the table and take a seat across from her. I'm not sure if it is really my fault that she spilled her food, but it feels like it is.

"Don't worry about it," she says.

I pick up my fork and stare down at the plate for several seconds and realize I'm not even feeling very hungry at the moment.

"Something wrong?" Danielle finally asks me.

When I look up, her eyes are focused on her plate of food. I stare at her a moment, unsure of how to answer her question.

"Blake," she says.

"Sorry," I shake my head slightly as if to clear it that way.

"You said you wanted to talk," she reminds me.

"I do," I say. "I just don't really know where to begin. The last couple of weeks have made everything so... complicated again."

"I know," she agrees. "You just have to be patient."

I nod at the familiar refrain. It's the same thing she said over and over since Amanda returned.

"Eventually—" she says.

"Everything will work itself out," I finish the sentence for her. "I know."

"You just have to give it time," she says.

"I'm not so sure," I say. "Something has changed. She is like a different person now. Or I am. I don't know. I can't talk to her or anything. Hell, I feel like I don't even know what to say to you anymore either."

"What?" she says.

"You know what I mean," I say. "It's like you're avoiding me."

"I've been giving you some space," she says as she leans back from the table.

"I'm not blaming you," I say. "I know you mean well,

but things feel so different between us right now and I just don't know how to make sense of that."

"Blake," Danielle says and places her hand on top of mine. "Stop."

Her words make me quit talking and pay attention to her.

"Worrying like this won't help anything."

I let out a deep sigh and nod my head in agreement. Danielle is right. Her lips curl into a smile as I stare into her eyes. I lean forward a few inches but she gets up from her seat.

"I better get going," Danielle says as she drops a crumpled napkin on her tray of half-eaten food. "We can talk some more later tonight if you feel like it will help."

"Okay," I say. "Sorry."

"Don't be sorry," she says to me as she picks up her tray. "You have nothing to apologize for."

"This can't be easy for you," I say.

"Blake," she sighs. "I think I'll live."

She turns away and walks toward the garbage can and dumps the food in the wastebasket and places the dishes in a plastic tub on the counter. On her way back to the hallway, she pauses beside me. Danielle leans down and kisses me softly on the cheek before she leaves me sitting alone with my uneaten plate of food in the empty mess hall.

I eventually take a few bites of food, but I'm really not very hungry at the moment. Stitch sniffs the air as if to detect if there is still food that is on the table that is above his head. He lifts his front paws slightly and lets out a timid whimper to remind me that he is still hungry. I set the plate down on the floor and he scarfs all of it down in less than a minute. Then he looks up at me, licking his lips, and waits to see if I have anything more to give.

"You can wait until lunch," I mumble.

He lays his snout on my leg and nudges my hand while growling playfully. I scratch the scruffy hair on top of his head. His tongue laps at my hand and then I stop petting him and wipe the dog saliva off with a napkin.

"You always have to ruin it," I tell him.

He wags his tail.

Idiot.

I retrieve the plate from the floor and place it on the tray and then get up to return the dirty dishes. Stitch runs along beside me, pausing to sniff the floor as I drink the last of my coffee.

"Alright," I say. "Let's go out for a walk."

His ears perk up at the familiar word. He follows me out of the cafeteria and we exit the blast doors into the vast tunnel that leads to the surface. Then I follow him as he trots along, wagging his tail, sniffing the ground in search of something in the dark tunnel of solid rock.

The lights hanging above my head flicker for a fraction of a second and I look up at the bulb directly above me, unsure if the light had actually gone out for a moment or if I just imagined it.

Something groans in the distance. I take my eyes off the

light and look down the tunnel again. The sound is probably just a change in pressure in one of the pipes hanging from the ceiling. Stitch stops in his track and sniffs the air.

I know the dead can't get through the steel doors, but there is still something about being in these dark tunnels that makes me uncomfortable. The air in here feels damp and cool. Moisture clings to the wall and occasionally drips down on me.

I listen closely and hear the faint sound of the dead clawing and pounding against the steel door at the far end of the tunnel. The hairs on my arm stand up and a chill runs down my spine.

"Hurry it up," I urge Stitch.

He turns and looks back at me, then returns to searching for a rock to piss on. Finally, the mutt lifts his leg and sprays the wall with a trickle of urine and turns around to sniff it before trotting back.

"Let's go," I say and turn back toward the entrance to the facility. I try to ignore the dark thoughts that follow me around like the sounds of the dead in the tunnel.

But they will always be there.

CHAPTER FIVE

There is a lot to be thankful for here. Even if things aren't exactly easy, at least we're not living in constant fear. Sometimes just a hot shower and changing into some clean clothes is enough to make the world feel normal again. However, we enjoy a level of comfort that even makes me uncomfortable sometimes.

I know how quickly things can change.

On a hook next to the door I keep my pack. It's always ready to go and so am I.

Just in case.

President McGrath assured us that there have been no incidents inside the Cheyenne Mountain Complex since the outbreak began. But still, things can happen very quickly and when you least expect them. If that ever happens here, I will be ready for it.

I collapse onto the creaky bed in my cramped living quarters. My eyes stare at the old horseshoe hanging on the wall beneath the clock that tells me it's a little after five in the morning. Even though I'm still tired, I have too many thoughts running through my mind that would keep me awake.

In my mind, I play back the conversation with Danielle from a few minutes ago and dwell on every detail and nuance of it. Sometimes the things she doesn't say are just as important as the things she does.

Then I start thinking about Amanda. I wonder if I seem as different to her as she seems to me.

Then I feel guilty for worrying about my feelings at all.

There are so many things that are more important to deal with still. There will be time for my personal problems later.

But what if there isn't.

I remember when this all started. That was my biggest regret. Not putting the important people in my life first.

Here I am doing it all over again.

What the hell is wrong with me?

I don't even know what is right or wrong anymore. It feels like any choices I make will only end up with a horrible outcome.

The tight walls of the tiny room seem to get closer with each minute. I need to get out of here and away from my nagging thoughts. I get off the bed and open the door. Stitch follows me as I step out to the hallway without even realizing where I am going. For a moment after I close the door, the dog and I just stand there staring at each other.

"We should do something productive," I say to him.

He cocks his head to the side slightly.

"Let's see if Claire found us a cure for all this," I sigh.

Stitch wags his tail.

The hallways are still empty this early in the morning. Stitch trots along beside me beneath the aura of halogen bulbs, sniffing along the cracks at the bottom of the doors.

I take several turns without thinking much about where I'm headed. Then I stop when I realize I'm not sure where I am.

The Cheyenne Mountain Complex is really more like a dozen different three-story buildings on springs, linked together by a complex webbing of tunnels. The similar look of the corridors makes it easy to get lost, especially since we haven't been here very long.

I wander around until I find myself standing outside the glass window of the makeshift laboratory that has been set up for Claire and Doctor Schoenheim. There is no sign of Doctor Schoenheim, but Claire is already awake and staring into a microscope.

Maybe she is still awake.

Since we got here the woman hardly seems to sleep. It wouldn't surprise me at all to find out that is how she rests, using a microscope as a pillow. She finally lifts her head away from the eyepiece and sees me staring at her in the hallway.

I hold my hand up and offer an awkward smile. She raises her hand and waves for me to come inside.

I'm still not even sure why I decided to come down here. I didn't mean to bother her. Hell, I didn't even want to talk to her, but now that I'm standing here like an idiot and she invited me in, I guess I don't really have a choice. I open the door and go into the lab as she jots something on to a sheet of paper.

"Sorry," I say. "I didn't mean to bother you."

"It's fine," Claire says. She tosses the pen down and tilts her head from side to side to stretch it out. "I need a break anyway."

"Have you been up all night?" I ask her.

She glances at the clock on the wall.

"I guess I have been," she says. Claire rubs her eyes and yawns while she stretches her arms above her head. I walk over to the desk covered in papers with sloppy notes and calculations scrawled all over them. None of it makes much sense to me at all but I didn't really expect it to.

"Is there something you wanted to ask me?" Claire wonders.

"Oh," I say. "Not exactly. I just wanted to see how it was going."

My eyes settle on the papers scattered on the desk again. I try to get some idea what the notes are about but I get nowhere.

"It's not going well," she says abruptly. "I'm getting

nowhere trying to develop a biological weapon to use against these things."

"What about Doctor Schoenheim?" I ask.

Claire shakes her head.

"He's getting worse every day."

"We'll keep looking until we find what we need," I say. "We're doing everything we can."

"Well we need to be doing more," she snaps as she scrawls over the last equation that she had noted on the paper.

The sudden edginess in her response catches me off guard and I stare at her in shock. She slaps the pen down on the desk and lets out a sigh as she buries her face in the palms of her hands as though she is about to cry. Then just as quickly she lifts her head again and regains her composure.

"Sorry," she says. "I'm just so frustrated."

"It's fine," I say. "I get it. There's a lot of pressure on you."

Claire takes a deep breath and picks up her pen from the desk again, then brushes a loose strand of her reddish hair behind her ear.

"I didn't mean to take out my frustrations on you," she forces her lips into a smile. "I know you're doing the best you can."

"You're just tired," I say. "You're pushing yourself too much. You need to rest."

"You're probably right," Claire says, but she lowers her eyes and begins reviewing her notes again.

I can tell she is feeling uncomfortable and realize it was a mistake to bother her. All I did was make her feel more stressed out than she already felt. I leave the desk and open the door to the hallway before I pause and look back at Claire once more.

"We'll get the medication," I say once more. "I promise."

Claire looks up and gives me another forgiving smile.

"Thank you," she says.

I close the door and head back down the long hallway a mile beneath the surface of the earth where the dawn is presently approaching. By now, Chase and the rest of the crew will be awake and gearing up.

The thought of another long day scavenging around the mountains of Colorado doesn't exactly sound appealing today. The only thing worse would be staying inside and having to face all the things I want to avoid.

I round the corner to head back to my room to grab my pack, but then I hear the sound of a door closing. I look up from the floor and stop abruptly when I see Amanda. As she turns and sees me she freezes for a moment, too.

I manage an awkward smile. Her eyes dart from side to side, then settle on the floor.

This is how it is now. Uncomfortable.

I take a few slow steps towards her as I try to think of what I should say.

"Good morning," I say to her.

She tries to smile but can't even make eye contact with me. I know she has been through hell and I've done things to destroy her trust, but I also still hold on to this ridiculous hope that somehow we can put things back together.

Without really thinking it through, I wrap my arms around her. Her body seizes up and she abruptly pushes me away from her. She takes a step back and looks over her shoulder as if she is debating to run the other way down the hall.

"Sorry," I say.

"Don't touch me again," Amanda whispers.

"Sorry," I repeat. "I shouldn't have... I should have known..."

"No!" she says loudly as she retreats a few feet from me, her hands across her chest, clutching the folds of her shirt.

The door beside me opens suddenly. Lacey eyes me suspiciously and then glances at Amanda and back to me again. Her fierce eyes stare at me as she takes her hand off the pistol holstered to her thigh.

"Everything okay?" she asks.

"We're fine," I say.

"I wasn't asking you," she snaps at me.

Stitch curls up a lift and lets out a little growl at her.

Lacey looks down at the dog coldly and then he stops growling and sits down close to my leg.

It's not that I don't appreciate everything this woman

did to help Amanda survive, but I don't really like her very much at all. She seems a little off. I have no doubt that she went through a lot, too, but she is different. Amanda seems understandably afraid, but this other woman... She just seems like she wants nothing to do with any of us.

"I'm fine," Amanda mumbles softly. "I just got a little scared."

Lacey stands in the doorway a moment longer, then she retracts her head and slams the door.

"I need to go," Amanda says.

She tries to quickly walk by me.

"Hang on," I nearly try to grab on to her to keep her from walking away, but realize that would just be a mistake. "Amanda. Wait."

She takes a couple of steps away from me, but then she stops. She doesn't turn around but stands there and waits for me to speak again. I'm still not even sure what I should say.

"I have to leave now," I say. "But I'll be back tonight. Maybe we can talk."

She stands silent and frozen in place.

"I just want to talk to you," I say again.

"Okay," she says after a long pause. Then she resumes walking down the hall again without looking back.

"My life is so fucked up," I mutter to myself.

The despair I feel after talking to Danielle and Amanda both this morning is enough to make me look forward to getting out of here now. I grab my pack and rifle from my room and head for the blast doors with Stitch on my heels.

The dog trots along beside me, wagging his tail in excitement because he knows we're heading outside. The outside world may not be safe anymore, but even a stupid dog can sense that is where he actually belongs.

CHAPTER SIX

"Bout fucking time you showed up," Chase says. His eyes follow me as I walk to the trunk of the Tahoe and release the latch. "I was just about to leave without your ass."

"I'm not in the mood for your shit today," I say as I toss my pack in the back of the vehicle. "Let's just get the fuck out of here."

Scout eyes me closely from the passenger seat as I get behind the wheel and close the door. I glance over and notice a sheet of paper in her hands. Stick figures scrawled in colorful crayon across the page. She folds it up and tucks it into the liner pocket of her jacket.

"You doing okay?" she asks me.

"Just peachy," I say without bothering to hide my hostility.

"This place will do that to you," Lana says from the

backseat. "After a while, everyone starts to go a little stir crazy. I'm surprised we haven't all killed each other yet."

"It's just a matter of time," Scout says. She smirks to let me know she is only being sarcastic.

I turn the key and start the ignition. The lights flick on automatically and illuminate the vehicle in front of us in the dimly lit tunnel. Chase seems to be taking his sweet time getting going now, probably just to piss me off even more. I lay on the horn a couple of times. A moment later the taillights flick on and the engine turns over. Chase rolls down the window and casually sticks his arm out the window, raises his hand up, and gives me the finger.

"I should shoot those goddamn fingers off, too," I mutter.

"You're not that good of a shot," Scout teases me.

I give her a stern look. She is just trying to get me to ease up a bit.

"I'm just fucking with you, Blake," she says. "Relax."

I let out a long sigh. We start driving through the dark passageway. Light and darkness oscillate through the windshield as we pass beneath the yellow bulbs strung from the ceiling of the tunnel.

We pause at the entrance to the tunnel and wait while the security teams get ready to open the door. Gunfire erupts outside the door as the SGR-A1 sentry guns detect the motion of the undead and take them out.

A moment after the turrets go quiet, the doors rumble and a sliver of daylight fills the opening. Scout slips a pair of sunglasses over her eyes as the light washes over our faces. I follow Chase through the doors, both vehicles treading on the bodies of the dead that have fallen in the road. As soon as we clear the entrance, the doors reverse direction and close behind us as the security team makes sure that all of the dead stay outside.

"Another day in paradise," Lana says.

"Where are we heading?" I ask.

"Going to head south," Scout says.

"We've already been south," I say. "Pueblo burned to the ground."

"Not Pueblo," Scout says. "Chase wants to go farther east."

"There's like nothing there."

"La Junta. Riverdale. Las Animas," Scout says. "We haven't gone that way before. Chase said there are a couple of hospitals there. Satellites confirmed there was visible undead activity in the area. It's worth a shot."

"I guess," I say. It does sound promising, but I've learned not to get my hopes up by now. Even with all the resources available to us, finding a specific kind of medication in this wasteland has proven to be more challenging than any of us would have guessed.

"If only we had known he needed this medication when we rescued the doctor in Missouri," I say to Scout. "We could have tracked some down."

Scout thinks about it as she stares through the windshield.

"I'm pretty sure Lorento knew," Scout says.

"What?" I ask.

"Yeah," Scout says. "Back in Iowa City Lorento insisted on going to check out a pharmacy in this mall we were at. I hadn't met the doctor yet so I didn't think much about it at the time, but now it makes sense. That was when Bishop captured her. For all I know, she might have even found some. It might have been in her satchel when she died. If I had just known..." Scout trails off.

"Why wouldn't she say something about it?" I wonder.

"I just think she didn't want anyone else to know."

"Why?" I ask her.

"She didn't trust anyone," Scout says. "Besides, if we knew there was a chance that Bishop might find out if we were captured and she wasn't about to take that chance."

"Son of a bitch," I mutter. "All this time."

She nods her head quietly.

"I never put the pieces together before now. I suppose I can't really blame her," Scout says. "She just did what she thought she had to do to stop Bishop and Arkady."

She turns her head and her eyes gaze out at the overgrown brush along the side of the road while I steer through the debris and remains on the ground. A bright flash to my right catches my eyes as I make the turn onto the highway. I take my foot off the accelerator and let the vehicle slow for a moment. My eyes check the side of the road and my rearview mirror to look for the source of the light.

"What is it?" Lana asks. She stops scratching Stitch on the head and swivels in her seat, raising up her rifle.

Scout turns her head away from the window and looks at me, too.

"I thought I saw something," I say.

"What?" Scout asks me.

"It's okay," I assure them. "Probably just the sunlight reflecting off a piece of glass or something."

I force my eyes to stop checking the mirrors and focus on following Chase through the abandoned cars and corpses ahead of us. I don't want to risk rear-ending him. Then we'd really have a problem.

Even though most of the buildings in Colorado Springs were destroyed when the government firebombed the city in the early days of the attack, countless dead still shamble down the streets. They never go away. No matter how many we destroy, more and more come back to take their place. It makes it hard to believe we will ever see the end of them.

The highway peels away from the city and I settle back into my seat to get a little more comfortable for the long ride. I flick the switch on the door and lower the rear window down enough for Stitch to poke his head out the opening. Then I open the front window a crack as well and take in a deep breath of the cool morning air.

Scout slumps down in her seat and closes her eyes. In the rearview mirror, I see Lana staring at the mountains on the right side of the road.

As crazy as it sounds, we're all relieved to be back out here.

Lana is just happy to be able to see the sun again every day after months inside the bunker.

As much as Scout cares about Stevie, it's been hard on her since his father died. Now she is everything to the kid, and even though she won't admit it, I can tell that she feels the burden of it whenever she is inside the mountain.

And I just want to be out here to avoid the problems I don't know how to solve.

As much as I know I will need to work through things with Amanda eventually and figure out where we go from here, right now it's just easier to focus on what we have to do today. But whenever I find myself in the middle of a long silence, the thoughts I am trying to get away from creep back into my mind.

I stare at the massive slope of Pike's Peak and notice the first layer of snow for the year covering the summit.

"It's still August and there's already snow," Scout says. Her words spill out suddenly. She turns her head and looks at me, her top teeth dig into her lower lip.

"It's not unusual," Lana says. "Especially up in the mountains. Haven't you ever been by mountains before."

"No," Scout says, her head turning to look at the monolith again. "We never really had the money or time to do much traveling."

"Well, it's nothing to worry about," Lana assures her.

"It will snow some evenings and melt by noon the next day."

Scout settles back into her seat again.

We all know winter is coming soon. However, no one is certain about how much that will change our circumstances.

Some speculate that the dead will all just freeze once the temperature drops enough. This would seemingly make it safer out here, but driving around these snowy mountain roads might be impossible without plows to clear them.

Then there is the fuel. We try to limit our usage as much as possible, but more than half of the stockpile inside Cheyenne Mountain has already been depleted since the outbreak. When that runs out then we will lose the heat, the lights, and the water.

Statistically, our odds of making it through the winter are not very good at all, so we need to find a way to stop these things right now. That's why we are still out here every day. It's our only hope.

The brake lights flare in front of us, and I slow down behind Chase. The Tahoes come to a stop on the highway. I lean to the side to see what might be the trouble, but aside from several abandoned vehicles, the road looks fairly clear up ahead.

"Blake," the voice of the young Marine blares through the radio on the seat beside me. I pick it up and key the mic.

"What's the problem?" I ask him.

"See that grey hatchback up ahead?" he asks. "The one with the hood up."

I lean to the side again to see around the other Tahoe and spot the car.

"Yeah," I say. "I see it."

"There's somebody behind it," he says. "Two males."

My mouth feels dry and I take a moment to swallow before I hit the button and respond.

"Did you get a good look at them?" I ask.

"Not good enough," Chase says. "Can't tell if they're armed. Could be a trap."

I glance over at Scout. We've been through this before. Sometimes it goes well, and sometimes it goes very bad. There is just no way to know. Scout stares at me for a moment before giving me a slight nod.

"We'll check it out," I radio back to Chase.

"Copy that," Chase says. "We'll cover you. Stay frosty."

I leave the keys in the ignition and the Tahoe running while Scout, Lana, and I step out onto the road. Even though everything around us seems to be still, I take another moment to scan the overgrown brush along the highway before we advance on the hatchback.

Chase opens his door as we approach and then the others follow his lead and exit the vehicle. They take up positions around the vehicle to keep an eye out for any signs of trouble. Chase eyes the hatchback warily, his gun propped in the open window.

"Don't do anything stupid," he warns me again.

It reminds me of something Quentin used to say, except his voice did not have all that animosity in it.

I know Chase would rather not take chances like this. That's why he lets us handle it instead.

It's probably better this way.

He has a bad habit of killing people.

I raise the rifle as we close in on the vehicle, ready to pull the trigger at the first sign of danger. We angle across the road and use an abandoned red sedan about twenty yards from the hatchback as cover when we make our approach. After we get to the sedan, we duck down behind the hood and observe the hatchback again.

For a long minute, everything is quiet.

"Stay the fuck back!" a man stammers from behind the car. Even though he tries to sound like a badass, the man hiding back there could not hide the fear in his voice.

Over the hood, I spot a pair of blue eyes blinking beneath the brim of a trucker hat. Long, unruly strands of dark brown hair stick out from the sides of the cap and cover his ears.

"I've got a gun," he says as he raises the barrel of a hunting rifle up and props it on the hood. "Don't think for a second I won't defend myself."

"Take it easy," I call out to him.

"We're not going to hurt you," Scout adds.

The man adjusts his grip on the rifle and squints an eye as he shifts the barrel slightly and seemingly attempts to make a decision about which one of us he should aim at. I doubt he even has any bullets for that gun since he didn't open fire on us already. Even if that's most likely the case, I wouldn't bet my life on it.

"Are you guys all alone out here?" Scout asks him.

"Shut up!" the man barks. "Just get the hell out of here and leave us alone. We ain't done nothing to you."

Scout stands slowly and sets her rifle down on the hood of the sedan. She raises her hands up and shows the man her empty palms. The man shifts the rifle barrel and points it at Scout, but opens his squinted eye and pulls his head away from the sight.

"I just want to talk," Scout says. "Maybe we can help you."

"Help me?" he says as though the concept of people helping each other were the craziest idea he had ever heard.

"Yeah," says Scout. She steps out from behind the cover of the sedan and moves a little closer to the man, even though he still has the gun pointed on her. "We have a safe place."

"Safe place," the man laughs. He looks Scout up and down, takes in her clean clothing, weapons, and body armor. His demeanor changes. He blinks and I can see a faint flicker of hope flash in his eyes.

"It's true," Scout says. "You can come there with us. What's your name?"

There is a long pause.

"Andrew," he finally says.

"I'm Scout," she tells him. She turns and gestures back to us. "Those are my friends, Blake and Lana."

His eyes dart over to find us watching him down the barrels of our weapons.

"What do you say we all put our guns down now?" Scout says.

There is another long silence as the man looks around and realizes that if we really wanted to kill him we would have just done it already.

"All right," Andrew nods. He shifts his rifle so the barrel points towards the sky. He gets to his feet and comes out from behind the hood of the car.

"See?" says Scout. She looks back and gestures with her hand for us to lower our weapons. "Nobody needs to be pointing guns at each other."

"I didn't have any goddamn bullets anyway," Andrew says.

Son of a bitch. I knew it.

Andrew pats the dust off his dirty jeans and glances at the others guarding the vehicles up the road. Another unarmed guy in a cowboy hat appears from behind the hatchback as well. He has overgrown shaggy blonde hair and an unkempt beard that makes it difficult to judge his age from this far away, but I'd guess they were both in their mid-twenties.

"This is Shawn," Andrew says and halfway raises a hand to lazily gesture to his companion.

Shawn lifts a trembling hand and smiles with an open

mouth as though he wants to say something. At the last moment, he decides against it. He lowers his eyes and tucks his hands into the pockets of his jeans anxiously.

"Sorry about all that," Andrew says. He looks around and makes eye contact with each of us. "Not many people out here willing to help anybody these days. We really appreciate it."

"Nobody got shot," Scout says. "That's all that matters."

We've learned to be careful on the road. After all, we have met all kinds of people already. Sometimes when we weren't careful, it came back to haunt us. The statistical data would probably say that most people who are still alive out here are dangerous. It's not likely they've survived this long without doing something questionable along the way.

My gut is telling me that these guys seem decent enough. Nothing about them at all strikes me as sinister. Every once in awhile the world still surprises me and makes me think that everyone out there might not be hopelessly lost.

CHAPTER SEVEN

"Can I have a word?" Chase whispers to me and Scout. He eyes the two survivors in their ragged clothes while they gulp down bottles of water next to the Tahoe.

We move by the rear vehicle to be out of earshot.

"What's their deal?" he asks.

"They say they've been alone in the mountains since the beginning," Scout says.

"Just the two of them?" Chase says.

"They were on a fishing trip and when they heard what was happening they stayed as far from everything as they could."

"That's bullshit," he says. "I don't buy it."

"They seem pretty harmless," I say.

He glances at me quickly out of the corner of his eye, then sighs and stares at the two men again.

"We'll split them up in the cars," he says. "I doubt they'll try anything. Ask some questions. We'll see if their stories line up."

"All right," I agree.

Chase leaves Scout and me by the rear vehicle and returns to the other SUV.

"Blondie," he barks.

"My name is Shawn," he says.

"Whatever. You're riding with them," Chase says and jerks a thumb in our direction. He grabs the rear door handle and opens it up and his eyes settle on Andrew. "You're riding here."

Shawn locks eyes with Andrew for a moment and opens his mouth to speak, but Andrew presses his lips together and turns to climb into the backseat beside Hawk.

"Let's get moving," Chase says as he closes the door. "We already wasted enough time out here."

Moments later we're all back in the trucks and rolling down the highway again. Stitch pokes his head over the backseat from the cargo bay and wags his tail. Shawn flinches at the sight of the mutt, but when he sees Stitch panting excitedly he reaches out his hand and pats the dog on the head.

"I can't believe you guys have a dog," Shawn smiles and scratches the dog on top of his head. It makes me glad to see Stitch spark happiness in others. Stitch lets his tongue hang out the side of his mouth and looks up at Shawn with his stupid, adoring puppy dog eyes.

"Most people would have eaten this little guy a long time ago," Shawn laughs. "I'm just kidding."

His dark humor chases the smile from my face and I turn my eyes back to the road.

"Where were you guys heading?" Scout asks him.

The smile falters from his face and he stops petting Stitch and turns to look back at Scout sitting in the front seat.

"We were just looking for people," Shawn says. "We'd been surviving alone out there for months. We thought maybe everyone was dead until we saw you."

I turn and glance at Scout. She locks eyes with me and I can tell she isn't sure what to make of his response either. It is possible to survive for over five months in the vast wilderness of Colorado without running into anyone, but it's not easy.

"Where are you guys heading?" he asks. "You got some kind of safe place?"

"Right now we're heading to a town to look for some medicine," Scout tells him. "We have a place that is safe. There are lots of other people. People working together to stop what's been happening. We'll take you there with us if you want."

When I glance in the mirror, I see Shawn with his mouth hanging open.

"You know what's been causing all this?" he asks.

"Sort of," Scout says. "I mean, we have people working on it. Scientists."

A cry from behind me draws my gaze back to the mirror. His filthy blonde hair hangs in front of his face, his hand cupped over his lowered face. I can't be sure if he is laughing or crying for a moment.

"You okay?" Lana says and places a hand on his back.

"Yes, sorry," Shawn says. "It's just... I never expected to hear news this good. It doesn't seem real."

"It's not all good news," I mutter. "Things are still pretty bad. The government is holding on by a thread."

"Government?" Shawn says. "We still have a government?"

"Barely," Lana says.

"This is incredible," Shawn sits back in his seat and takes the news in.

As bad as things seem to us, I guess it must seem much worse to people that are still out here all alone. Most people probably assume there is nothing left to save.

Maybe it's better that way.

Statistically speaking, the odds of us turning this around are astronomical. Deep down I know this, but I can't bring myself to say it to the others. I don't even like to admit it to myself.

The radio emits static on the dashboard.

"This is our exit coming up," Chase says.

We follow the other vehicle up the exit ramp and onto a small country road heading east toward the morning sun.

"What are you guys trying to find out here?" Shawn asks. "It looks like you got plenty of weapons and shit."

Scout thinks about how she wants to answer for several seconds. Even though she is one of the most honest people I've known, Scout knows we should be getting information instead of giving it.

"We don't have everything we need," Scout says.

Shawn waits expectantly for her to go on, but she pivots.

"What did you do before all this?" Scout asks him.

"I was a bartender," he says. "Nothing special."

"What about your friend?" Scout says.

"He sold cell phones," Shawn tells her.

"How do you know him?" Scout continues questioning him.

"We just grew up together," Shawn says. "Up in Fort Collins."

I tune out the rest of the conversation and return my focus to the road. The small town in the distance creeps closer and I spot the dead bodies shambling up ahead. My muscles start to feel tense in anticipation of danger. I ignore the small talk and focus on the weaving in between the mangled bodies that wander on the highway.

"Here we go," I say.

"I can shoot," Shawn says. "If you give me a gun."

"Not a chance," Lana scoffs.

"Come on," he says. "I want to help."

Even though he sounds sincere, there is no way we'd even consider giving him a weapon.

"Just try to stay close and don't get eaten," Scout smiles at him.

"You're kidding, right?" he asks.

I accelerate to keep pace with Chase in the first vehicle and follow him as close as I can without risking a collision. The small town is overrun with the dead. Dozens of them wander down the main road and every side street. All of them notice the noise of our vehicles approaching and converge on our location.

This is going to get messy. I can already tell.

"Holy shit!" Shawn panics as he sees the dead all around us. "They're everywhere."

"There it is!" Scout points to the pharmacy a block away.

"Be ready to move as soon as I stop the truck," I say to no one in particular.

Chase plows into a couple of corpses standing at the entrance of the parking lot. One of the decrepit bodies flips over the roof his Tahoe and crashes down on top of the hood of ours and shatters the windshield. A web of splintered glass and blackish blood blocks my view.

My foot slams the brakes and the truck screeches to a halt. By the time I shift the engine to park and fling open the door, everyone else has already climbed out of the Tahoe.

Stitch barks at the building as he races toward the closed door. Gunshots ring out in the still morning air. In between each report, I hear the moans of the dead, hundreds of them, getting louder as they close in on our position.

I raise up my rifle as I backpedal toward the entrance of the pharmacy. I point the barrel at a man with a head of bright orange hair coming straight at me. My finger pulls the trigger and the bullets hit him twice in the chest before the final round blasts through his head. With the parking lot momentarily clear, I look over my shoulder to see Hawk smash through the glass door with the butt of his rifle.

"Come on," Hawk barks.

I turn and run through the shattered door and grab a shopping bag from the register.

"Five minutes," Chase warns us. "We'll hold them off."

Scout and Lana file through the door behind the two new guys and then direct them to head for the pharmacy counter while Chase, Natalie, and Hawk set up a defensive position beneath the overhang outside the front of the store.

Gunfire fills the air as we run through the aisles to the back of the building. We push through the doors of the pharmacy and I struggle to remember the name of the medication as I open the plastic shopping bag and start rummaging through cabinets and drawers.

"What are we looking for, man?" Andrew asks. "We can help."

I stare at the countless bins but still draw a blank on the name of the drug.

"What is it called again?" I ask Scout.

"Donepezil!" Scout yells.

The two guys start searching through the medications as well. The only sound is pills rattling inside the plastic bottles and the rapid firing of the assault rifles out front.

I shove some antibiotics with a name that I recognize in the bag. Then I notice some insulin and grab that as well. I don't know if it will still be any good, but at least it's something that might be useful.

The gunfire stops momentarily and I hear Chase yelling something at the front of the store but I can't understand what he is saying. They must be in some trouble up there.

"Forget it," I say. "We need to get out of here."

"I found it," Lana says. She emerges from between a row of shelves and holds up a bottle and grins. "I got it."

"Let's go," I say.

We abandon the pharmacy and run back to the entrance, but instead of getting ready to leave, I discover that Chase, Hawk, and Natalie are shoving a giant display rack in front of the open door instead.

"Give us a hand," Chase yells as we approach the entrance. He presses his back against the rack as the swarm of dead bodies reach the storefront and begin their assault on the other side of the fixture. "We need to reinforce this."

We push the checkout counter and a few racks over to the doorway and pile them up. At least fifty or sixty corpses wail and press against the barricade. It feels like it still isn't enough to even last the night, but for the time being it keeps the dead outside. We can make it stronger if we need to, but we aren't exactly planning on making a stand here. All we need to do is keep them from getting in here long enough to figure out a way to get us out.

CHAPTER EIGHT

"Check the back doors, Hawk," Chase says. "See if the alley is still clear."

"On it," Hawkins says. He swaps a fresh magazine into his rifle while he hustles toward the back of the building.

"We can't get back to the trucks," I point out. "There's too many of those things out there. We'd never make it."

"No shit," Chase gasps. He slumps against a rack of discounted movies and settles on the ground. Chase takes a deep breath and wipes the sweat from his brow. He is still sucking wind from moving all those heavy store fixtures.

"Did we get it?" he finally manages to ask me.

I know he means the medication.

"We got it," I smile.

"Now we just need to get out of here without dying," Lana says.

"That might not be so easy," Hawkins says as he comes back down the aisle. "Alley is full of those fucking things."

"So what now?" Shawn says.

"You guys going to call someone on that thing?" Andrew says, pointing to the satellite phone that Chase is removing from his bag. "Get someone to come get us out of here."

"That's not how it works," Chase says. "We're on our own."

"Fucking great," Andrew says.

"Just chill the fuck out," Chase snaps. "Let me think."

The dead moan and claw at the pile blocking the entrance. I consider the options as I look around the store again.

"We can wait them out," I finally suggest. "At least until they thin out."

"That'll take hours," Hawk says. "Hell, it could take days. You really think this pile of crap will keep them from getting in before then?"

"Then we'll make it stronger," I say. "You got any better ideas?"

Hawk scoffs and shakes his head.

"He's right," Chase agrees with me. "We're stuck. For a little while anyway."

Chase gets to one knee and looks at the door. The pile of fixtures wobbles back and forth slightly.

"Let's finish securing the entrance and get out of sight," Chase says.

We spend ten loud minutes shoving merchandise off the shelves and dragging screeching fixtures over the tile floors until the barricade is strong enough to last the night and every corpse outside is riled up and moaning. They crush their bodies against the building trying to get to the source of the noise. Then we grab our stuff and head for the stockroom so we draw less attention to ourselves.

"I thought we had satellite surveillance," I say.

"We did," Chase says. "There weren't this many of the damn things twenty-four hours ago."

"Then what the hell happened?" Scout asks. Her voice shakes with frustration.

"Maybe there were a bunch of them inside somewhere," Chase says. "Maybe they followed someone else here. I don't fucking know."

"Could be worse," Lana says as she stares at the inventory on the shelves against the wall. "At least we have plenty to hold us over here."

Lana reaches up and pulls a case of beer off the wall. It's cheap and warm, but it's still beer. She pulls open the cardboard and removes a six-pack.

"I'll take one of those," Natalie says.

"No she won't," Chase says.

Natalie stops smiling and gives Chase a questioning look.

"Not out here," he says to her. "You need to stay sharp."

Natalie looks back at Lana holding the beer in her hand and shakes her head.

"I'll take one," I say.

Lana hands me the bottle, then I gesture for another and she plucks another one out of the cardboard box and hands it to me as well. I walk over and give one to Natalie, and ignore the dirty look Chase gives me as I twist off the cap of my bottle and take a long swig. Natalie waits a moment, then tucks the bottle into the pouch on the side of her backpack.

The dark mood in the room makes me start to feel deflated. I drop my pack on the floor and take a seat on a couple of large boxes. Even though no one is complaining, none of us are particularly happy to be stuck inside here right now. While we know that we can make it out of here alive eventually, we'd all be happier back in the safety of the bunker.

"How long did you say those things will stay out there?" Shawn asks.

"Could be a day. Could be a week," says Natalie. "No way to know."

"Hell," says Hawk. "They might never leave unless something draws them away."

"Better tell everyone back home we won't be coming for dinner tonight," Chase says. He takes out the satellite phone and calls into the communications team at Cheyenne Mountain to give them a situation report.

Scout paces anxiously along the wall beside me. Her

eyes stare at the floor as she considers our situation. None of us want to be here, but nobody wants to get back more than Scout. The thought of not being there for Stevie tonight is probably making her crazy.

"Who's Comet?" Andrew asks when Chase disconnects the line.

That's the radio callsign for Cheyenne Mountain. Chase used it even though he was on a secure line. I can understand why. Even though Andrew and Shawn seem decent enough, being cautious is still the best option.

"You'll know when you need to know," Chase says as he puts the phone back into his pack.

"I know you guys don't know us," Andrew says. "But you can trust us."

"It's nothing personal, man," Chase says as he zips his bag closed.

Andrew takes a few steps to close the distance between him and Chase.

"I served, too, you know..." he whispers. "We both did."

"Good for you," Chase says. "But I still don't give a shit."

Andrew takes a step back and looks at Shawn over his shoulder and shakes his head in frustration.

"Don't mind, Chase," I say. "It takes a while for him to warm up to everyone."

Andrew looks at me, then back at Chase, then turns and walks away.

"We shouldn't have left the cabin," Andrew mutters to

Shawn in a voice that was quiet enough to act like he was trying to be discreet, but loud enough that he was sure Chase and the rest of us would hear it, too.

Really, I can't blame the guy. Chase is an asshole. Even if he has some fucking medal that says he is a hero, it doesn't make him a good person.

Andrew stares down at the floor and listens closely when Shawn leans over to whisper something to him. Suddenly Andrew jerks his head up and the two lock eyes. Then Shawn shrugs and mumbles something else. Andrew looks at him for a long time, then he nods his head. The two men finally look over and notice the rest of us watching them talk.

"We might have a way out of here," Andrew says. "Come on."

We follow Shawn and Andrew back out of the stockroom. They lead us down an aisle filled with office supplies. Shawn grabs a couple of roles of packing tape then turns and scans the toys on the opposite side of the aisle.

His eyes settle on a large rectangular box on the bottom shelf with a remote-controlled monster truck inside. Shawn hands Andrew the box and then heads for the next aisle. He snags a pack of a few packs of batteries as he rounds the corner.

"Those things aren't just going to follow that," Hawk says skeptically.

Shawn just ignores him as he scans the shelf. He locates a small, cheap boombox on the shelf and picks it up and examines the box then stacks it on top of the other box that Andrew has cradled in his arms. Then Shawn walks up to the cash register and selects an album from a dusty bin of discount compact discs.

My eyes notice something familiar and I reach into the bin and pull out a disc. It's The Cure album.

I hold it up for Lana to see.

"You have got to be fucking kidding me," she sighs.

"It's a classic," I shrug.

"I'm going to throw that damn thing out again," she says and then she follows the others to the back of the store.

On my way back, I notice some cans of dog food so I grab one for Stitch and stick a bunch more in my bag and grab a plastic bowl off the shelf. Stitch looks up at me and cocks his head to the side, then his tongue flicks out and he licks his chops.

We return to the stockroom and Shawn unboxes the remote-controlled truck and inserts the batteries. He does the same with the boombox. Then he unwraps the compact disc and places it in the player.

I pry the lid off the container of dog food and turn it over and watch as the hunks of meat and gravy plop into the bowl below. Stitch dives in and chews with his mouth open so we all have to listen to the wet smacking sound of him eating. I do my best to ignore the disgusting noises but I have to admit the sound makes me nauseous.

"I'll need to get up on the roof to see what I'm doing,"

Shawn says. "I should be able to draw them far enough away to give you plenty of time to make it to the trucks."

"Pretty good plan," Scout says.

"Not bad," Chase admits.

"Just don't leave me here," Shawn says.

"Someone just needs to stay behind and cover him," Andrew says.

All of us look at each other silently, but no one volunteers.

"If you want to let me have a gun, I'll do it," Andrew offers.

"That ain't happening," Chase shakes his head.

"I'll do it," Lana says.

I'm still a little skeptical this will actually work, but it sure beats sitting here for the next couple days. Shawn heads up the stairs to the loft with Lana.

Chase checks the back alley through a peephole in the stockroom door.

"They're far enough away from the door," he tells Andrew. "I'll open it and you drop the thing outside."

"This is never gonna work," Hawk rolls his eyes.

"Ready?" Chase says.

Andrew nods. As soon as Chase opens the door, Andrew hits the play button on the boombox and drops the truck in the alley. Chase slams the door the second Andrew is back inside. A fist abruptly pounds on the other side of the door. The first chords of a classic rock song can be heard through the metal door.

"Is that Aerosmith?" Hawk says.

"Yeah," smirks Andrew. "Seemed appropriate."

Steven Tyler howls and beckons the dead to walk. I exchange a glance with Scout and we both smile. It turned out picking up these guys was a pretty good idea after all.

The music fades as the monster truck rolls away from the door. Chase presses his face close to the peephole again.

"Holy shit," he says. "It's actually working."

Andrew boasts with a broadening grin.

"Of course it's working," Andrew said.

"Let's get ready to move," Chase says.

We check our weapons and ammo quickly before we get ready to run. I walk over to the door to the sales floor and open it a crack to look at the entrance. One or two of the dead still claw at the barricade, but it sounds like most of them have moved away.

"We're good up front," I call to Chase.

He pushes through the alley door and raises his rifle as he steps outside. The rest of us file out behind him. Once I step out into the alley, I can still hear the faint music in the direction of the road. I turn and run the opposite way.

We pass by the drive-thru pharmacy window and then round the corner and head along the side of the building toward the parking lot. I pause for a split-second to glance back at the doors to see if Lana and Shawn have made it out yet, but they're still inside.

Several corpses come at us from the yards of the adjacent houses on our right. A few more wander down the lane from the front of the store. Chase raises his weapon and cracks the first stiff that gets in his way in the face with the butt of his rifle. Hawk shoves another one in the chest as it lunges at him. The thing backpedals, stumbles over the curb, and flops onto the grass.

We reach the front of the building and keep running for the vehicles. Stitch is already at the back door with his tongue hanging out. He pants anxiously while he waits to be let in the back.

Most of the dead took the bait, but about ten of them still linger near the entrance. They don't even notice us running across the parking lot as they bang and moan at the barricade.

We almost make it to the cars before one of the things happens to turn around. It wails and stumbles after us. The rest of the things stop pounding and turn and follow it along.

I glance back the way we came. Even though we made it to the cars, there is still no sign of Lana and Shawn. I get a sinking feeling in my stomach that something has happened to them.

"Get the truck started," Chase barks at me. "We'll hold them off."

I nod and climb behind the wheel and fire up the engine. I check the mirror and notice Natalie starting the other Tahoe. Chase and the rest of our team open fire on the dead coming at us from the store.

Still no sign of Lana and Shawn.

I notice the dead that had followed the monster truck up the block have noticed the sound of the engines the gunfire and started heading back in our direction.

"Come on," I mumble to no one in particular. "Let's go, Lana."

Finally, the two of them emerge from the side of the building. Lana is limping along beside Shawn, her arm slung over his shoulder. The dead trail just a few steps behind them.

"Hurry the fuck up!" Chase yells.

I feel helpless sitting behind the wheel as the dead close in around all of us. Panic sets in when I realize that Lana still has the medication in her bag.

"No," I whisper out loud as I watch the dead catch her from behind.

Shawn tries to shove the corpse away, but another one grabs him from behind. Before he can shrug himself free, teeth tear into his neck. Blood spurts into the air until his hand clamps over the wound.

The thing must have bit into his artery.

Within seconds, Shawn releases his grip on Lana and lets her fall to the ground as he goes down to a knee. Lana lets out a scream as the dead encircle her. Before she disappears beneath them I notice something in her hands.

She is holding a grenade.

"No," I whisper.

I watch as she pulls the pin. Then she disappears into the horde.

"They're right on us!" Natalie yells.

The horde is heading straight for us. I look the other way to see even more descending on the pharmacy from the other side of town. If we don't get out now we're going to die here.

"Come on!" I urge Scout as she opens the door.

Stitch starts barking his head off in the backseat when the first corpse reaches the car and bangs against my window.

I slam on the gas as soon as Scout gets her door closed. Since the dead are blocking the parking lot entrance, I have to drive over the grass embankment and the sidewalk to get across to the road.

I speed across the street and cut through the lot of a gas station and out onto an empty road. There is a loud blast behind us as the grenade explodes. Then I press the pedal to the floor and accelerate to sixty miles an hour until we reach the highway at the edge town. I glance back to make sure that Chase is still behind me. When I see the other Tahoe there, I relax a bit, but then I notice the thin trail of smoke drifting up to the sky.

I bang a fist against the steering wheel.

We lost the medication and we lost Lana.

CHAPTER NINE

"You okay?" Scout asks me. The sound of her voice registers, but I stare at the road, my mind thinking about everything that just happened.

"Blake," Scout says.

"Yeah," I snap back at her. "I'm fine."

I turn my head to see her watching me closely through narrowed eyes. She knows I'm lying. The truth is I feel like I'm about to lose it. All I can think about is all the people I have watched die. It never ends.

"I should have made her give me the medication when she stayed behind," I mutter.

"You had no idea that was going happen," Scout says. "The same thing could have happened to you just as easily."

"It was all for nothing now," I mumble. "She died for nothing."

Scout opens up her mouth as though she wants to refute my statement, but she can't find the words. She closes her mouth again and lays her head back against the headrest and looks out the passenger window at the vast meadow.

In the rearview mirror, my eyes find Andrew. He'd been so quiet that I'd nearly forgotten he was back there. His glassy eyes stare vacantly out the window. He is probably feeling guilty that they came along with us and now his only friend is dead.

We get back on the highway and head for home. The drive seems even longer with the heavy silence of grief that we carry with us. It isn't just the devastation of losing someone else I had come to care about.

Lana had survived so much already.

She helped rescue McGrath. The woman was a real fighter. A hero.

But in the end, it didn't matter. It was still her time.

If death can come so suddenly to take away someone as tough as Lana, it can happen to any of us.

Maybe we should have tried to wait them out. Maybe it wouldn't have made a difference.

I know that wondering about these choices does no good, but I can't help but feel burdened by the consequences of our decisions for the rest of the drive back to Cheyenne Mountain.

As the sun begins to sink below the mountains, we pull through the heavy steel doors and follow the long tunnel to the entrance of the facility. We park the vehicles in the outer lot and head through the heavy blast doors. Danielle is waiting for us with Stevie just inside the entrance as usual, but the smile falls from her face when she notices that Lana did not return with us.

I walk over and wrap my arms around her and pull her close to me.

"I'm sorry, Blake," she whispers.

Scout hugs Stevie beside us and puts a smile on her face for him.

"I'm so happy to see you," she tells Stevie. "Come on. I want to hear all about your day."

She pulls him along by the hand and the two of them head back down the hall to the barracks.

"Are you okay?" Danielle asks me.

"Yeah," I lie.

Her eyes shift over to the newest member of our group. Andrew stands in the entrance, examining the giant blast doors.

"This is Andrew," I say.

Andrew looks up at the mention of his name and comes closer.

"Hey," Danielle smiles. "Welcome to Cheyenne Mountain."

"This place is unbelievable," Andrew says. "There's power."

"Yeah," I smile. "And hot water."

"No fucking way," he says.

"Why don't you come with me to the clinic?" Danielle says. "We'll get you checked out and then you can get cleaned up."

She holds out her left hand to show him which one of the hallways to take and then Andrew starts walking. I'm anxious to head back to the room and get cleaned up myself, but then Danielle looks back at me.

"Would you mind coming along?" Danielle asks. "There's something I need to talk to you about."

For the first time, I notice how anxious and tired she seems. She wrings her hands together. Dark circles rim her bloodshot eyes.

"Sure," I agree.

We walk a few steps behind Andrew. I can tell she doesn't seem to want him to hear what she has to say to me.

"What's going on?" I ask her. "Is everything okay?"

She hesitates for a moment, and then her hand finds mine and she looks me in the eyes and smiles.

"Yeah," she says.

I can tell she is trying to make it seem like everything is fine. She doesn't want me to panic. But it's not like her to try to hide something from me.

"Danielle..." I say.

"I don't want you to panic," she says. "People are getting sick."

"What do you mean?" I ask her.

"It's spreading," she says. "Faster than I thought, too."

"Hold on," I say. "What is it?"

"I'm not sure," she says. "Some kind of bacterial infection, I think. We're still waiting on some test results."

"But it's nothing too serious, right?" I ask her.

Danielle hesitates.

"No," she says. "Not yet anyway. But I'm concerned."

"What can I do?" I ask her.

"We are going to need more antibiotics," she says. "I'm already running low and if more people get sick then..."

Andrew glances back over his shoulder at us and Danielle points to a hallway on the right.

"Just do what you can," Danielle says.

"We're trying," I tell her.

"I know," she says. "But we really need them now."

We stop in front of the clinic. All the chairs in the waiting area are full and several people are standing around the front desk. The handful of volunteer staff on duty scramble around anxiously and try to deal with the patients.

The scene inside the medical center makes me nervous.

The Cheyenne Mountain facility has a small clinic, but they are not generally equipped to deal with anything more than minor injuries and the occasional headache. The doctors on staff at the nearby military base never made it here. A nurse practitioner and Danielle are the closest people here to a doctor.

"I'll talk to the others," I assure her. "We'll figure something out."

"I know you will," Danielle smiles and then puts her arms around me and lays her head on my chest. Her affection takes me by surprise after our conversation this morning. After a moment, I put my arms around her as well.

"Just promise me you will take care of yourself, Danielle," I say. "If you get sick—"

"I'll be fine," Danielle says. "Don't worry about me."

She unwraps her arms from around my waist and then looks at Andrew.

"Come on," she says and opens the door for the medical bay. "This will just take a few minutes."

He waits a few seconds and looks a little reluctant to go inside, but eventually, Danielle's smile persuades him and she follows him through the door. I wave goodbye to her and then turn to head back down the hall.

Before making my way back to the room, I grab a quick bite to eat in the mess hall. Even though it's been a hard day and I'm tired, it still takes a while for me to drift off to sleep after I lay down in bed beside Stitch.

I am jolted awake some hours later by the blaring of an alarm. Stitch jumps off the bed and lets out a growl. It takes a moment for me to get my bearings. I glance over and look at the clock to find out several hours have passed. Danielle isn't in the room.

I throw the blanket off and get to my feet. I snag my go-bag off the nail beside the door and grab my rifle off the table. Then I crack open the door a few inches and scope out the hallway.

An alarm blares.

"This is an emergency," drones a robotic female voice. "Containment teams please report to storage bay four. All other personnel initiate lockdown protocols. This is not a test."

I step out of the room and then Stitch sniffs the air and lets out a long, deep growl. He smells the dead.

Another door pops open and Scout peers out into the hall, a handgun ready in her hand.

"What's going on?" she wonders.

"I don't know," I tell her. "Just keep Stevie inside and keep the door locked."

She hesitates for a moment. I know she wants to help, but the best thing she can do is to keep an eye on Stevie. Scout finally nods and closes the door again.

I take a moment to tap on the door across the hall and then open it. Amanda is sitting beside Lacey and her kids on the bed. Lacey holds has a rifle pointed in my direction.

"Easy!" I say.

Lacey lowers the rifle slowly.

"I just wanted to make sure you're okay," I tell them. "Stay inside. Keep the door locked."

Down the hall, Chase and Natalie emerge from their room with their rifles at the ready.

"I'll be back," I tell Amanda and Lacey before I close the door again.

"What the fuck is going on?" Chase growls as soon as he sees me. He rubs at his groggy eyes and tries to focus on me. Nothing like this has happened since we came here.

"Sounds like we're on lockdown," I say.

"Lockdown?" Natalie says.

The female voice drones the same message as before.

"Maybe we should get back in the rooms," I suggest.

"Fuck that," Chase says. He glances at Natalie standing behind him. "You ready?"

Natalie slaps a magazine into her rifle and gives him a nod, then the two of them begin to advance down the hall.

"Where are you going?" I ask.

"I'm going to make sure the lab is secure," Chase says.

"Wait," I plead.

The two of them just keep walking away.

"Damn it," I curse.

Stitch takes off after the two of them as well. No one ever listens to me.

I jog down the hall to catch up with them to help make sure that Claire and the doctor are safe. Maybe I will be able to locate Danielle, too. I get the feeling that she was right to be afraid. Things here are already much worse than they seem.

CHAPTER TEN

We reach the main entrance to find the blast doors are still secured. But there is no one around.

Nothing like this has happened since we arrived.

The lockdown protocols posted on signs around the facility advise us to secure ourselves in a room and lock the doors until the all-clear is given.

In spite of this, we head through the empty hallways.

Most of the people inside here have very little experience in dealing with the dead. There is a good chance they will need our help.

I catch up to Chase and Natalie as they reach the lab. Chase rattles the door as he tries the locked handle. He bangs a fist against the heavy wooden door.

"Claire!" he says loudly.

A few seconds later, Claire opens the door for us and we slip inside the lab.

"What the hell is happening out there?" asks Claire.

Doctor Schoenheim continues to tinker with some kind of device at the desk as though he is completely unaware of anything going on around him.

"I don't know," Chase says. "We're going to go take care of it. You stay put in here."

He removes his sidearm from the holster and puts it on the desk in front of Claire.

"Anybody other than me comes through that door you know what to do."

Claire nods.

Chase heads back over to the door and grabs the handle. He inches the door open and recons the hallway before raising his rifle moving ahead.

The alarm blares again, a strobe light flashes, the female voice issues another warning.

Stitch crouches down low to the floor and leads us down the hallways. The corridors on this level seem mostly empty.

It makes me still wonder if this isn't some kind of drill.

Maybe it's a mistake or something.

We make our way toward the staircase to head down to the lowest level where the storage bays are located. Gunshots reverberate through the vents of the facility. It is impossible to tell which floor the dampened shots are coming from.

We open the door and start to work our way down the flights of stairs. At the bottom level, Chase opens the door and we see a rifle on the ground and streaks of blood on the tiles and along the walls. A man screams somewhere as the alarm blares the lockdown warning repeats again.

I cover behind us as we move down the hall. Stitch lets out a low growl as he slinks cautiously down the hall beside me.

We reach the closed door of storage bay four and there is no sign of the containment team. Stitch reaches the door first and sniffs around the doorway and then his lip curls into a snarl. Chase arrives at the door a second later and swats the dog away before he places his hand on the doorknob. Stitch whimpers and takes off down the hall the way we came.

"Hold up," I tell Chase. "Shouldn't we wait for the containment team."

"Good idea. You stay out here and wait for help," he says to me. "I'm going in."

"Wait," I insist.

The cocky bastard won't listen, though. He twists the handle and pushes his way through the door.

"Shit," I curse as I follow him and Natalie inside.

The large room is lined with rows and rows of shelves filled with cardboard boxes up to the ceiling. As I try to scan the aisle, I hear a moan off to my left.

I turn to look but Chase already has his rifle raised and fires a pair of shots at a corpse on the left. The deafening gunshots still echo off the concrete walls after the corpse drops to the ground. I clamp a hand over my ear and growl in pain, but then I freeze when Chase spins around and brings his rifle up and aims it at me.

His cold eyes are locked on me. A few weeks ago, I was the one pointing the gun at him. I doubt he will have the same reluctance to squeeze the trigger as me.

"No," I stammer.

"Get the fuck out of the way," he barks.

Someone tackles me to the ground in the aisle as Chase fires the rifle. It takes me a second to realize it was Natalie. She knocked me out of the way as a corpse was about to grab me from behind. A dead maintenance man collapses on the floor at my feet. His face slams against the concrete floor. Blood trickles out of a hole in his forehead as his lifeless eyes stare at me.

I turn to get up and spot another corpse coming around the other end of the shelves. The guy is wearing one of the steel blue jumpsuits that the warehouse workers wear. I raise my handgun and fire off several rounds, missing badly. Finally, a bullet punches the guy through the skull as Natalie fires from the floor beside me. The corpse lets out a groan and drops to his knees before he keels over. I listen for a few more seconds to see if I can detect any more of the dead, but the storage room is quiet again.

"I told you, you should have stayed outside," Chase says. "Fucking dumbass."

I turn around to find him standing over me. He holds a

hand out and Natalie reaches up and grabs it, and then he hauls her up off the floor.

"You should have waited for the containment team," I tell him.

"You think I was trying to shoot you or something?" he asks with a smirk on his face.

"The thought might have crossed my mind," I admit.

"Whatever, smart guy," Chase scoffs and shakes his head and holds out a hand. I let him help me to my feet again and then take a look around the room and at the bodies on the floor. There is still no sign of the containment team.

"Where the fuck are these guys?" Chase wonders.

"They sure do take their time," I agree.

"Maybe they're all dead," Natalie says.

We all look at each other then a series of gunshots echo through the bunker. With our rifles up we head back into the hallway. A man in a containment suit that was not there a few minutes ago stands in the hallway with a submachine gun dangling from his neck, his head uncovered and arms reaching for us. He lets out a snarl as Chase squeezes off a few rounds. The last shot hits the man in the head and he slumps against the wall.

"Guess we know what happened to the containment team," I say.

"It's spreading too fast," Natalie says.

"You're right. We need to contain this or we're going to

lose this place," Chase says. "Stick close to me and put down anything that moves."

Chase takes the lead and we step over the dead body in the biohazard suit and head down the hall. We have no idea how many more people may be infected by now. Hopefully, the lockdown procedures will keep most people in their rooms, but then again it didn't stop us from coming out here to find out what was going on.

Around the corner, a soldier in uniform hunches over another deceased member of the containment team. The soldier sits up, pulling a chunk of skin from the dead body and gnaws on noisily until Chase puts a round into the back of his skull. Natalie fires a couple of shots into the other body on the floor to make sure it doesn't get back up before we move on.

Four more of the dead are drawn out by the sounds of gunfire. They emerge from an open doorway up the hall. Chase stops advancing and we open fire on them as they spill down the corridor. I take aim at another member of the containment team and fire, sending a burst up his sternum and the last bullet hitting him in the forehead just above his left eyebrow. The bodies fall to the floor and we step over the splayed limbs as we advance down the hall.

We reach the end of the hallway and then it splits off in both directions. Chase glances back and wags his fingers to tell me he will head left. He swings around the corner checking the left passage, and I turn and quickly check the right.

I spot a body lying in a puddle of blood on the floor. It might be down for good, but I fire a round into it anyway just to be sure.

Another person screams ahead of us somewhere. A door slams. More gunshots.

I can't shake the feeling we might not be able to get control of this situation.

We move as quickly as we can toward the next corridor, following a set of bloody boot tracks on the floor. They lead us around the next corner and to another infected man in a containment suit. He moans and pounds his bloody hands against a closed door. Chase fires a pair of shots that drop the thing before it even notices us approaching.

On the other side of the door, someone cries. Chase grabs the handle and swings open the door. A woman shrieks inside. She cowers against the far wall of the darkened office. Her hand clutches a gushing bite wound on her neck.

"Jesus Christ," I sigh.

We lower our rifles slightly. The pleading eyes of the woman move between our faces. Her breathing is shallow and anxious.

"Please help me," she whimpers.

There isn't anything we can do for her with the amount of blood she is losing with each passing second. Even if we tried to carry her upstairs to the medical center, she probably wouldn't make it.

"I'm sorry," Chase says.

He raises his rifle.

Her eyes open wide with the realization that the end of her life is seconds away. She opens her mouth to say something. Maybe she is going to scream. But before she has the chance, Chase pulls the trigger.

It's the kind of thing I could never do even if it was necessary. I stand there staring at the body of the poor woman while Chase swaps a fresh magazine into his rifle.

"We need to keep moving," Chase says.

I think about Danielle and force myself to look away from the scene in the room and follow Chase and Natalie down the hall. We make our way to a staircase at the far end of the building with blood smeared on the steel door.

The alarm continues to blare. The monotone voice repeats the lockdown warning again. Strobe lights flash from the emergency lights along the hall.

We open the door and enter the stairwell without a sound. There are droplets of blood on the stairs. As soon as Chase rounds the first landing, a corpse moans and tumbles down the stairs after him. We all open up with the rifles and pepper the man. Stray bullets ricochet around the stairwell. My ears ring from the deafening noise of the gunshots inside such a confined space.

On the second floor, more blood streaks mark the walls. A balding corpse tries to lunge through the door as soon as Chase pushes it open. Chase grabs the handle to pull it shut again, but the head of the thing is already through the opening and the door closes on its neck. It snaps its teeth, blood spilling out of the thing's mouth every time it opens. Chase pulls the door as hard as he can as if he might just be able to separate the head from the body.

"Fucking shoot it already," he growls.

Natalie raises her gun and sticks the barrel into the open mouth of the man and squeezes the trigger. The back of his head explodes and he flops on the floor.

Finally, we push through the doorway, shoving the dead guy out of the way as we step into the hall. A pair of bodies are motionless on the floor in the hallway. A few of the overhead lights are shattered leaving the passage in semi-darkness.

Another corpse, a woman dressed in scrubs from the clinic with long dark hair stands in the dim light. The lower half of one of her arms has been eaten down to the bone.

My heart sinks into my chest. I don't want to believe it could be Danielle but I get this horrible feeling that it is.

Chase raises his weapon and gets the woman in his sights but I reach out and push the muzzle toward the ground.

"What the fuck?" he says.

"Hold on," I say.

He looks at the expression on my face and then at the woman down the hall and realizes why I don't want him to shoot.

"Oh shit," he says softly.

I leave him standing there and approach the corpse. She

raises her head as I get closer and aim the rifle at her face. The woman snarls and hurls herself at me.

It's not her. It's not Danielle.

I realize it a split-second before I pull the trigger.

Her head snaps back and she falls to the ground a few feet away from me. I stare down at the face of the woman for a long moment to be sure.

"It's not Danielle," I finally say.

"Come on," Chase says. "There might still be more of them around."

CHAPTER ELEVEN

Five more corpses surround the entrance to the medical center. The floor to ceiling glass is still intact, but the people inside panic every time one of the dead smashes against the windows.

The dead don't notice us approaching from behind them in the hall. We creep as close as we can to be sure that none of the people trying to keep the dead from getting into the clinic get caught in the crossfire.

From a few feet away, we make quick work of the corpses. A couple of rounds still puncture the glass. The bullets leave spiderwebs of cracks in the glass that is covered in bits of brain and splattered blood.

As soon as we clear the bodies and open the doors, I find Danielle and wrap my arms around her.

"I thought I lost you," I whisper to her. The anxiety I

had felt a few moments ago when I thought she was gone comes back. I struggle not to break down and cry.

"I'm okay," she reassures me.

The moment makes me realize, I've really come to love her. Whatever Amanda and I had before is gone now and there is no getting it back. I'd only been fooling myself in thinking otherwise.

"Blake," Chase says. "We need to make sure that's all of them."

I slowly release my grip on her. Even though it seems like we are getting the situation under control once again, I am still reluctant to leave Danielle.

"I'll be back soon," I assure her. I take out my sidearm and hand it to her.

We return to clearing the building. It takes a few more hours over checking each of the structures room-by-room before we are completely sure that there are no more zombies still lurking. By the time it is all over, the body count rises to a total of twenty-seven. Even though it was bad, the whole situation could have been much worse.

Still, the personnel inside the complex are concerned. President McGrath emerges from his command bunker to try to calm the anxious crowd of personnel gathered there to find out what is going on.

"Everything is under control," he assures them.

An unconvinced groan emerges from the crowd. A few people wave away the President's remark with a dismissive hand.

"We want to know what is going on!" a man with glasses wearing a white buttondown shirt and tie with a pocket protector demands.

Any authority the politician held as their leader is already quickly slipping away. Once people realize their leaders are powerless to protect them they are bound to start questioning the hierarchy.

"This might get ugly," Chase whispers.

"What do we do?" Scout asks.

"Someone needs to say something," I suggest.

Without a word, Danielle walks away from me. She works her way through the crowd toward the President, then stops when one of the secret service agents grabs her by the arm. She looks at McGrath and I'm not sure if she said something, but he nods his head and the agent lets her go.

"Excuse me!" her voice is louder than I'd ever heard it before.

The crowd of people quiets down a moment later.

"I know some of you don't know me," she stammers. "I help out in the clinic. What happened is not President McGrath's fault. If you want to blame somebody, you can blame me. One of the people that died was being treated. They were sick. Some kind of bacterial infection. I think it may still be spreading."

She lets that sink in as an anxious murmur overtakes the crowd.

"We're doing our best to treat it and get it under

control," Danielle continues. She pauses and thinks about her next words some more and says, "I'm doing my best. Until this is under control the best thing you can do is to..."

She looks anxiously at the crowd as though uncertain if she should say what she is about to say.

"I'm ordering a mandatory quarantine of the entire facility until further notice," she says.

"You don't have the authority to do that," a soldier says.

"Given the circumstances," McGrath says. "I'd say she does have the authority."

"I'm sorry," Danielle tells the crowd. "Stay in your rooms unless you notice any symptoms. If you feel dizzy, feverish, or nauseous, come to the clinic immediately."

The crowd disperses quietly. Some of them covering their noses and mouths slightly as though to lower their risk of getting sick. But the reality is, we're all trapped in here together. The odds that this will spread quickly are pretty high.

We make our way over to Danielle and McGrath.

"Thank you, young Lady," President McGrath smiles at Danielle. "I really appreciate what you did. Let me know if there is anything I can do for you in return."

"There is," Danielle says. "You can go back to your room and stay there. It might not seem like it, but these people cannot lose their leader."

The President seems to consider this for a moment. He reaches out and shakes her hand.

"I'm counting on you," he says. His eyes leave her face and he looks around at the rest of us. "And your friends."

"We won't let you down," Danielle assures him.

McGrath smiles and turns to head back inside his safe room followed by his security team.

Danielle looks up at me after the President is gone.

"We need that medicine," she says. "I don't know how long I can keep it together here if we don't get more antibiotics."

"We'll get it," I assure her.

"How?" she asks.

"We'll have to go to Denver," Chase says. "We don't have another choice."

A long silence follows his statement. No one wants to risk going to Denver, but we know we are out of options. It is a major city. Even if much of it was destroyed and it is overrun with the dead, there are still a lot of supplies because no one is crazy enough to attempt to go in there and get them.

"We can maybe try going farther east today," Scout suggests. "Some small towns out that way that they might not have bothered with."

"We have to face the fucking facts," Chase says. "If we want to find what we're looking for fast, our best bet is to go to Denver."

"No way," Scout shakes her head.

"I'm with Scout on this one," I say. "It's too risky."

"That's exactly why we will find the medication that the Doc needs there," Chase says.

"Three million people," I say. "Three million. That's the kind of numbers we'd be facing."

"You can sit this one out if you want, man," Chase says.

"I'm not saying that," I tell him.

"Then what are you saying?" Chase says.

I think about it for a few seconds.

"Won't we need some more firepower?" I suggest.

Chase considers it the idea for a moment, then he shakes his head.

"No," he says. "Just Hawk. The more people we bring out there the more likely it is that somebody fucks up and gets us all killed."

"None of them know what the fuck they're doing out there anyway," Natalie agrees.

I still don't like it, but I can understand their point of view. To me, it's all about improving our odds, but sometimes having the numbers on your side isn't the only thing that matters.

"I can't believe we're even talking about this. It's insane," Scout shakes her head.

"I'm not saying it will be fucking easy," Chase says. "I'm just saying we don't have any choice. If we don't get some of that medication soon then we're all just as good as dead anyway."

Everyone is quiet as his words sink in. We all know he's right.

Danielle looks at me and I can see the fear in her eyes. After the last few hours, I understand why she is afraid. Even though we got things under control right now, there is no guarantee that they will stay that way very long. Besides, I promised her we'd do everything we can.

We all agreed to go back out there because we know that our hope of defeating the dead hinges on getting the doctor what he needs to figure out a solution.

We might all die if we go to Denver, but it's just a matter of time before we all die if we don't. The massive amount of supplies the government stored here won't be enough to last all of us through the winter.

Doctor Schoenheim is our only hope. We need him to figure out a solution to turn this around right now.

"I don't like it," I say before I turn to look at Scout. "But I think he might be right."

"I know I'm right," Chase says.

"You can't be serious," Scout scoffs.

"We're running out of other options," I tell her. "We're running out of time."

"We'll stick to the suburbs," Chase says. "We can probably find what we need without getting within ten miles of the downtown area."

Scout looks down at Stevie. He stares up at her. It isn't hard to recognize the fear and uncertainty in his eyes. Just when he had started to feel safe this happens. Scout places her hand on his head and smiles.

"All right," Scout finally agrees. "I still say this is crazy."

"You don't have to go," I say. "We all know you've got Stevie to think about. No one will blame you."

"I'll never forgive myself if I stayed and something happened to any of you," Scout says.

"Alright then," Chase says. "Let's gear up."

Chase and Natalie head off to get ready to go, but Scout lingers behind for several seconds with me and Danielle. She bends down and wraps her arms around Stevie. Then she lets him go again, but he just stands there, holding Scout with his teary gaze.

"Are you leaving?" he asks.

"I am, kiddo," she tells him. "But I promise I will be back real soon. Stay with, Miss Danielle."

Stevie glances at Danielle and she smiles at him. She holds out a hand and Stevie lowers his eyes and slowly takes it.

"He'll be fine," Danielle assures Scout. "I'll take good care of him."

"I know," Scout smiles. "Thanks."

As much as I don't want to leave Danielle, I smile and hope she doesn't see right through it as I say goodbye.

"Don't worry," tells me as I wrap an arm around her and hug her tightly.

"I'm not worrying," I tell her. "We got this."

I let go of her and notice her smile that tells me she isn't buying a word of it.

"I wish I didn't have to leave you here alone," I admit.

"I'm not alone," she reminds me.

"You know what I mean," I say.

Danielle smirks and leans close and kisses me.

"I'll be fine here," she says. "But you need to get going. We don't have a lot of time."

I nod and let go of her hand. Then Scout and I head down the hall together.

"Maybe we'll have better luck out there today," I say to Scout. Even though I am trying to seem optimistic, I can hear the hopelessness in my voice as I say it.

"I sure hope you're right," Scout says.

We get back to the dorms and Scout heads inside her room to gear up. Instead of heading inside my room, I turn to the door across the hall and knock softly.

"It's me," I say.

The door opens a crack and Lacey stares out at me.

"You..." she says.

"Yeah," I say. She stares at me coldly. I try a smile, but the truth is this woman makes me kind of uncomfortable. She is someone I'd avoid completely if it wasn't for Amanda. The two of them developed a bond while they were out surviving together out there. I get that. But I kind of wish she would just go away now.

"Can I come in?" I finally ask.

Lacey steps back from the door to let me through. I push the door open a bit more and step inside. Amanda sits on the bed. Her eyes notice me and then she averts her gaze to avoid looking at me. She doesn't move or say a word to me.

"Amanda," I finally say. "I was hoping we could talk."

She doesn't respond. Her eyes stare down at her hands on her lap.

"I don't think she wants to talk," Lacey says. The tone in her voice gets under my skin.

"You know," I say. "I think I saw your kids down the hall. There is about to be a quarantine put into effect for the whole facility so you might want to get them."

She looks at me for a moment, then looks at Amanda.

"It's okay," I say. "I'll keep her safe until you get back."

Lacey gets up and silently walks out of the room. The truth is I have no idea where her kids are at. I am just trying to get rid of her. Once she is gone, I get up and close the door and lock her out. I notice the sound of the door being locked seems to snap Amanda out of her trance and she looks at me with anxious eyes.

"I have to leave," I tell her. "But before I go, I needed to talk to you."

I pause to allow her to say something, but she just stares at me. My eyes search for the woman I remember while I sit down on the bed across from her.

"I don't know if you're even listening to me or if any of this will make sense to you anymore," I say. "But there is something I need to tell you anyway."

I pause to take a deep breath. Even though I want to turn back now, I know I can't.

"Amanda," I say. "I'm so glad you're still alive. The moment I saw you again I knew it had to mean something.

I thought it had to mean that we were meant to be together again. That it meant we'd be able to someday go back to how things used to be when we were a family..."

The word catches in my throat and I have to pause to swallow before I can speak again. I notice a tear falls from Amanda's eye. Maybe she is listening after all. Maybe she knows what I am about to say as well.

"But now I know we can't go back," I say. "We will never be the same people that we were before. We can't even look each other in the eye. I can't keep pretending that somehow we..."

A loud banging at the door interrupts my sentence. Amanda flinches at the sound and then I lose her attention again.

"What the hell!" Lacey yells. "Let me in."

I know I'm out of time, but it's a relief to have said what I needed.

"I'm sorry," I whisper to Amanda. "I will always miss what we had."

I get up from the bed and unlock the door. Lacey barges in and gives me an accusing look, but I just ignore her as I step back into the hall and shut the door behind me.

It's time for me to go.

CHAPTER TWELVE

We load up on ammo and enough food and water to last us a couple of days in case we need it, and then we climb into the Tahoes and leave Cheyenne Mountain shortly after dawn.

Even though we slept half the night, the last six stressful hours we spent clearing the facility have left me feeling exhausted. We don't have time to rest anymore. Our trucks roll down the access road in the early morning light and then we turn and head north on the highway toward Denver.

Stitch pants loudly in the backseat. Scout nibbles on her fingernails as she watches the road from behind her aviator sunglasses. It's not typical for her and watching her do it makes me anxious, too.

"Scout," I finally say her name to get her attention. "You nervous?"

"Yeah, I guess," she says. She lowers her hand to her lap and clasps both of them together as though to keep either of them from getting away again. "I just have this really bad feeling in my gut this time. It feels... wrong."

I can understand why she might feel that way, but it still takes me by surprise. Scout isn't the type to worry. She has always stayed focused on doing what needs to get done.

"Is this like some women's intuition thing?" I ask.

She turns and cocks her head and shoots me an irritated look.

"What?" I laugh. "I don't know about that stuff. I'm a numbers guy."

"It just feels like something really bad is going to happen and there is nothing we can do to stop it," she says.

I watch her for a long moment. As soon as I look back to the road, she starts biting her nails again.

"You don't feel it?" she asks me.

"I don't know," I say. "I mean, it doesn't seem like we have any other choice."

Scout reflects on this for another long moment.

"I guess you're right," she finally says.

There is no way I want to have this conversation continue all the way to Denver. I fish around in the center console and dig out an old album by the Beastie Boys and put it on even though I know it will probably annoy Scout.

Except she doesn't even seem to notice it. She just

stares out the passenger window until we approach the outskirts of Denver. We stick to the highway as we drive by the same little towns we have already searched over the last several weeks. All of them already raided and stripped of anything of value.

Chase has to slow down ahead of me as the number of abandoned vehicles steadily increases with each mile. More of the dead begin to appear in the buildings alongside the road. They traipse after us through the tall weeds when they hear the engines of our vehicles.

I'd be lying to say I'm not anxious about what lies ahead of us, but I also realize I've been through situations that were just as bad, maybe even worse, and I'm still alive. If anything, I'm just feeling determined to get this done and get back as quickly as possible. We fought so hard just to find refuge inside of Cheyenne Mountain. There is no way I will rest until we manage to secure it once again.

The radio crackles to life on the seat.

"We're getting off here," Natalie says. "The road is blocked up ahead. We'll have to take the side streets."

"Copy that," Scout says. She takes her thumb off the push-to-talk button and sets the radio back down in the center console. "Here we go."

We drive up the exit ramp and I can see the mess of construction on the stretch of highway ahead that blocks us from going further. Orange barrels and barricades are scattered everywhere. Cars are lined up for miles in both directions heading into the city.

Chase takes a right at the intersection and we follow him down a road lined with desolate gas stations and fast-food chains. The windows are smashed up and the dead shamble around inside. Even after we locate a pharmacy around here, the odds of finding the medication there still seem pretty thin. It seems like these shops were all looted long ago.

We make a left turn and I spot a sign for a pharmacy up ahead, but then I notice the whole store is in ruins. It must have burned down. The roof caved. All that remains is charred bricks and rubble.

"Damn it," Scout sighs.

"We'll find one," I say. "They can't all be burned down."

Chase keeps heading straight for a couple more blocks, then makes another left turn and continues toward the city center. More of the dead start to appear on the road. We have to slow down to avoid hitting them, but we also need to make sure we keep moving to prevent them from swarming the vehicles.

Stitch lets out a whimper from the backseat, then barks as soon as one of the dead gets close enough to slam a hand against the window. Stitch lunges at them as if they might just get scared and go away. I would have thought that the dumbass mutt would have figured out that isn't going to work by now. Stupid dog.

"Shut up, Stitch," I tell him, but he just keeps barking as I drive. It is hard enough to keep from wrecking the truck without him making all that noise and making me even more anxious.

Chase swerves abruptly to the right to avoid several wrecked cars. He suddenly slams on the brakes, and then hangs a left turn. Hundreds of corpses wander up and down every street. Luckily, these roads are wide and lined on each side by factories and warehouses so it's easy to find enough room to drive around the dead.

I knew what we were getting into coming here, but at this moment it really dawns on me just how hard this will be. Even if we find a pharmacy that hasn't been looted, we will be lucky to even make it in the doors before these things are all over us. We really may not make it out of this one alive.

When I take my eyes off the road for a moment and glance over at Scout, I still see something unfamiliar there — fear.

"Look out," she yells.

I turn my eyes back to the road in time to see a corpse buckle as it strikes the front bumper.

"Shit," I mumble as I adjust the wheel to stabilize the vehicle.

"Keep your eyes on the road," she reminds me.

Chase takes a left and I can't help feeling like we're just going in circles. I sure hope he has an idea where we're going. After a few blocks, we enter another commercial district. Luxury strip malls line each side of the road.

Then I spot a grocery store ahead. I follow Chase into

the parking lot where a few cars covered in dirt sit amongst several dozen corpses. We pull up to the front of the store and jump out of the vehicles.

Stitch tries to follow me out of the car but I slam the door. He scratches at the window and barks angrily.

The dead are already closing in all around us. I realize the rifle might be too hard for me to manage at such close range, so grab my sidearm and fire at a woman in a yellow raincoat a few feet away from me. Then I sprint around the car and run behind Scout toward the door.

There is no way we can hold them off. We just need to keep moving and fighting them as we go. The entrance is locked, so Chase smashes through the glass doors. We step through, crushing bits of shattered glass beneath our boots.

Unfortunately, it seems like we aren't the first people in here since the collapse. Over the checkout counters, I spot mostly empty racks on each of the aisles. Our chances of finding what we need here just dropped significantly.

We run along the rows of checkout lanes and then we pass through the liquor department and head to the pharmacy in the back corner of the store. The moans of the dead echo off the tile floors as they make their way inside the building. I jump over the pharmacy counter and look around at the disarray of medications scattered around the room.

"Hawk," Chase says. "Help me hold them off."

At best we have a couple of minutes before the dead make their way to the back of the store. I start rifling through the scattered bottles of medication on the floor and on the counters.

I spot a bottle of Amoxicillin and grab it. The damn thing is empty. I throw it down again in disgust.

Chase and Hawk take up a position behind the counter and start laying down fire to suppress the advance of the dead. I spot a cardboard box with several more pill bottles in the corner and hustle over. My hands shake nervously as I check the labels and toss the first several containers aside.

Then I see the bottle of Donepezil. I stare at the letters for several seconds, but I am still unable to believe my eyes. I actually found it.

"Get ready to move," Chase says.

I get to my feet and look around. There isn't much else to search through. We may not have found enough antibiotics but at least we got the dementia medication that we have been searching for weeks to find.

"Let's go," I yell.

I pick up a metal stool from the floor and swing it at the glass of the drive-thru window. The grass cracks. I swing it again and it punches a hole in the glass. I climb on the counter and kick away more of the broken glass. A pair of corpses just outside moan and reach for me through the hole in the window. Natalie and Scout fire at them as I keep clearing the way.

I jump down into the alley and start shooting at the corpses to hold them off while the rest of them make their way outside. The dead come at us from every direction. As soon as I take one down, another appears from behind the trailers in the alley or from the corner of the building.

My mag runs empty so I quickly swap to the rifle slung over my shoulder. I raise my gun and fire at the dead coming at us as I start heading around the side of the building. After we take out a few to thin their numbers, we make our way back to the truck. Even though many of the dead are still hunting us inside the grocery store, a couple hundred are shambling through the parking lot toward the sounds of gunfire.

"Just make a run for it," Chase tells us when he sees me slowing down.

We don't have any choice. Every second, more of the dead converge on our location. If we don't get to the vehicles and get out of here right now, there will be no escaping the growing horde.

I fend off the dead goth teenager that lunges at me by shoving it to the side with my forearm, and then I sprint for the trucks. We avoid shooting at the dead so as not to hit the vehicles. Instead, I just do what Chase is doing and use my rifle as a bludgeon to knock down any corpses that get in my way.

We are almost at the Tahoes.

Ten feet from the door, a pair of grimy hands seize my arm.

I jerk my arm to try and free it from her grip, but the hands stay clamped on and the dead woman with long blonde hair just moves with me. Her open mouth searches for some flesh to devour.

Out of the corner of my eye, I realize a tall man in a gray suit reaches creeps toward me from the right as well.

They're closing in on me.

In desperation, I reach up and grab the woman by the neck with my free hand and pull her to the side and shove her into the dead guy in the suit. The two of them fall to the ground.

I glance around and see Scout struggling with a corpse that must weigh twice as much as her at the back of the truck.

Someone yells behind me. It could be Chase, maybe Hawk.

There is no time to look back right now. They're all over us.

I raise the rifle and take aim at the enormous guy as he tries to bite Scout.

For once, my aim is perfect. The round hits the guy in the temple with the first shot and he collapses on the ground.

Someone else curses and screams behind me. I whirl around and see Hawk on the ground, pinned beneath a handful of corpses. Chase is beside him and yells at Natalie. She stands next to the open door of the Tahoe, as the dead close in around her. At the last second, she hops behind the wheel and slams the door.

Chase bends down and tries to pull Hawk free. Before

he can, another corpse grabs Chase from behind and takes him to the ground as well.

There is nothing else I can do for them.

I sidestep toward the truck and raise the rifle. My finger squeezes the trigger and the bullets tear through the dead. Even though I try to keep my aim high enough not to hit Chase or Hawk, I know I am still taking a chance. The bullets pepper the bodies of the dead. One of the rounds manages to find a home in the back of the skull of the dead man on top of Chase and he immediately goes limp.

I stop firing and fling open the door of the truck. Another corpse reaches for me and I have to swat his arms way as I climb inside and slam the door. Scout is already in the passenger seat, her face and chest covered in blackish blood and gore.

More gunshots draw my eyes back to Chase and Hawk. They both are up off the ground and racing for the other vehicle and fighting their way through the gathering crowd of the dead.

"You okay?" I yell while I shove the keys in the ignition.

"I think so," she stammers.

The engine turns over and I slide the transmission into drive. Chase and Hawk dive into the backseat and Natalie hits the gas. The tires wail as she speeds down the road with the door still wide open.

The rotting corpses from all over the area swarm the parking lot now. They bounce off the hood of the Tahoe as I speed toward the street. The frail bodies explode from the high-velocity impact. One of the dead flips onto the hood. The body cracks the splintered windshield even more before it rolls over the roof and crashes to the ground behind us.

Tires squeal as we hook a sharp turn out of the lot and speed the hell away from this place as fast as possible.

CHAPTER THIRTEEN

"I got it," I say to Scout. "I got the medication."

Her eyes search my face for a moment as though deciding whether to believe me or not. She takes a deep breath as she recovers from our escape.

"You did?" she says.

I nod. The corners of her lips bend upwards.

"Did you find any antibiotics?" I ask her.

"No," she shakes her head.

"Those are much more common," I say. "Shouldn't be as hard to find."

The radio beside me comes to life and I hear Chase saying my name.

"Blake!"

I grab the radio and key the mic.

"I hear you," I say. "I got the medication for the doctor."

Chase keys the mic again, and I hear cursing in the background.

"That's great, man," he says absently. He seems so preoccupied that I'm not even sure he really registered what I said. Something must be wrong.

"Is everything okay?" I ask him.

There is a long pause before he transmits again.

"Listen," he says. "One of those things got Hawk."

I exchange a glance with Scout.

"I'm alright," Hawkins grumbles in the background.

"Just keep applying pressure on it," Chase tells him. "You're going to be okay."

"Which way am I going?" Natalie yells.

"I don't fucking know, Nat," Chase snaps. "I'm kind of busy back here. Blake!"

"What?" I respond.

"Did you guys find any antibiotics?" he asks.

"Negative," I tell him.

"Natalie found a small bottle. That's probably not going to be enough, is it?" he says.

Before I respond, I take a long moment to consider it. We barely made it out of the grocery store alive. We very likely will still lose Hawkins, too, by the sound of it. I want to call it quits, but I know we don't have enough antibiotics.

"No," I finally say. "We're going to need more."

"Copy that," Chase says. "We'll locate another pharmacy."

The line goes quiet and I set the radio back down in my lap. Scout picks up her rifle and starts reloading her guns. I pass my weapons over to her to get them ready as well.

Stitch opens his mouth and starts panting loudly in the backseat. Every time I have to swerve to make a turn or avoid the dead, the idiot dog loses his balance and falls down to the floor.

My heart is still thumping in my chest when I see a pharmacy up ahead. The adrenaline rush has me shaking anxiously and dripping sweat. But we still have to do it all over again.

"Here we go," Chase says over the radio. "On the left."

"Copy," I tell him.

I breathe a little easier when I notice that the parking lot surrounding this pharmacy is surrounded by a wrought-iron fence. A handful of corpses still shuffle over the faded yellow lines on the pavement out front. Nothing blocks the driveways, but at least the partial perimeter will force the dead to go through one of two entrances. These can act as choke points that make it easier to slow the dead down. It will buy us a few more minutes at least.

A few months ago, I would have just seen a store. Now how I visualize everything has changed. Everything has a tactical value. It's starting to become second nature to me.

The second we pull to a stop, we exit the vehicles. Stitch climbs into the front seat and lets out a whimper as I slam the door and he realizes he is going to be locked in the car again.

"Sorry buddy," I mumble as he stares at me through the glass.

"You guys go in," Chase yells. "We'll hold them off."

I run over and help pry open the sliding door. The inside of the store is a mess. Carts loaded with merchandise sit in aisles. Trampled boxes of food are scattered around on the floor. But there is still a lot here. All of it covered in a layer of dust like it hasn't been disturbed since the first days of the outbreak.

We run to the pharmacy counter at the back. Outside, the guns rattle as Chase and Natalie keep the dead away as long as they can. I flip open the swinging door on the counter and start digging through the medicines with Scout. In the fairly well-stocked pharmacy, we find what we need quickly and load up with as much Amoxicillin and Cephalexin as we can.

We did it. And we're still alive.

I feel a wave a relief as Scout and I run back to the front of the store. We're not home free yet, but we're almost there.

"Got it," I yell as soon as we step through the door into the afternoon sunlight.

Chase and Natalie keep firing at the dead pouring into the parking lot. They don't make a move to get into the vehicles.

That's when I realize our mistake. There are too many

of the dead coming through openings in the fence. It would be impossible to drive back out now.

"We can't get out of here," I say.

"Shit," Scout curses.

"Got any ideas?" Chase yells in between shots.

I look around but unless we plan on running for it, I don't see any way to escape. When Chase stops shooting and glances at me for a moment, I shake my head.

"Well, we can't stay out here," he says. He shoulders his rifle and pulls open the car handle. "Natalie! Give me a hand!"

Natalie stops shooting and helps him get Hawkins out of the car. I open the back door and let Stitch out of the backseat then all of us head back inside the pharmacy.

We shove the automatic doors closed again and flip the locks as the dead reach the entrance. They press their decrepit faces against the glass and moan at us inside the store.

"We're really starting to make a habit of this," Natalie smirks.

I turn around to find her sitting on the cash register. Chase reaches into the beverage cooler next to the checkout and grabs some bottles of water. He twists the cap off one and hands it to Hawkins, then hands another to Natalie.

Hawkins gulps down half the bottle before he exhales loudly and wipes the sweat off his forehead with his sleeve.

I notice the bloody bandage on his forearm for the first time and he catches me staring at it.

"Don't worry," Hawk says. "I'm not gonna die anytime soon."

I try to smile, but I never quite make it there. We all know by now that he does not have long.

"Not here at least. That's for damn sure," he laughs. "So you guys better figure out some way out of here."

"What do you think?" Chase says. "Maybe we can look around and see if we can find a remote control car. Give that trick another shot."

We looked around the store while the dead pounded away at the doors. Unfortunately, this pharmacy didn't carry any remote control toys. We didn't find much of anything that might serve as some kind of decoy or distraction.

"Looks like we're gonna be stuck here for a while then," Natalie sighs. She turns and looks at Hawkins. "Sorry Hawk. At least you got me here to keep you company."

"I'd say I'm still a lucky guy then," Hawkins smiles.

All things considered, he seems to be handling this unfortunate turn of events better than I'd have expected. Being fearless when death is so near and inevitable certainly makes me respect him even more.

"Goddamn it," Chase says. He presses some buttons on the satellite phone.

"Something wrong with it?" Scout asks him.

He holds up a finger as he puts the phone to his ear again. A moment later, he looks at the display again.

"Damn it," he growls.

He hangs his head and sighs. He stares at his hand with three fingers while he rakes his other hand through his hair as he contemplates something.

"What is it?" Scout asks him again.

"No one picked up at Cheyenne Mountain," he said. "I tried to call again, but the battery died."

"Died?" Scout says.

"It didn't charge all the way last night," Chase admits. He gestures vaguely with his mangled hand. "With all that shit going down."

"They didn't pick up, though?" Scout asks.

"Didn't I just fucking say that?" Chase growls. "Jesus."

He gets up and paces a few feet down the aisle. His head tilts back and he lets out a sigh as he gazes up at the rafters overhead. Then he turns around again.

"Sorry," he says to Scout. "I'm sure everything is probably fine there. We've only been gone like eight or nine hours."

I'm not really so sure, but it's not like we are able to do anything about it right now anyway. It seems like we're going to be stuck here for a little while.

We keep quiet and out of sight in the back of the store and wait for the dead to go away while the sun sinks and the world outside grows darker. Except the dead don't seem interested in going anywhere.

Even if we could leave now, there is no way we would want to attempt the drive back at night. It wouldn't be so bad to wait out the dead in here, but everyone feels uneasy that we aren't in contact with Cheyenne Mountain after what happened there this morning.

I try not to think about it too much. Maybe it's good that I'm so tired after hardly sleeping last night. As soon as the night settles in, I manage to doze off sitting in a plastic lawn chair while listening to the dead moaning outside.

Sometime later, I wake up with a sore neck. I look around and notice everyone is asleep except Chase. He sits there with his rifle in his hands and his eyes on Hawkins.

I rub my eyes and yawn before I tilt my head from one side to the other to stretch my neck muscles. Then I look at Hawkins again. At first, I thought he was sleeping, now I'm not so sure. The big man is slumped against a rack. His head lolls to one side. It doesn't seem like he is even breathing.

I turn to ask Chase about him, but then I notice the syringe that Chase has in his hand and the bottle of medicine on the floor. He follows my gaze and then he looks down seems to rediscover the needle he holds in his hand.

"It's better this way," he says. He lets the syringe fall to the floor.

"Is he..." I say.

"Yeah," Chase says. "His fever... He was delirious. Rambling. Wouldn't shut up. Those things out there must have heard him."

133

He sniffs as he gets to his feet. For a long moment he just looks down at Hawk in silence. Then Chase removes his knife from the sheath and he walks over and grabs hold of Hawk. I look away as Chase puts the blade into his brain so Hawk won't get up again.

Chase returns to his lawn chair and sits down with the bloody knife still clenched in his fist and stares at Hawkins again.

"Why don't you get some sleep?" I offer. "I'll keep an eye on things."

Chase doesn't say anything. Just sits there for a few more minutes. Then he stands up and walks toward the back of the store. I'm not sure if he left to sleep or if he just wants to be alone, but he is gone for several hours while I sit alone and wait for Scout and Natalie to wake up again.

Scout opens her eyes first and spots the dead body near her and jolts upright. Her eyes quickly look around the pharmacy.

"It's okay," I tell her.

Scout's eyes settle on me and then she lets out a sigh and collapses back into the lawn chair. She combs her hair back with her fingers and looks at Hawk again.

"When?" she asks.

"A few hours ago," I tell her. I decide to spare her any of the details that I know. It won't make it any better.

"That isn't the only bad news either," I say and jerk my head toward the front of the store.

The dead are not going away.

The crowd still moans and claws at the front doors. By the look of it, a few of them may have wandered away from the building a little bit, but the whole area is still crawling with them.

Natalie opens her eyes as well and jumps in her chair when she sees Hawk. Then she glances around.

"Where's Chase?" she asks.

"I think he wanted to be alo-" I start to say.

"I'm right here," Chase suddenly appears at the end of the aisle. "Just been trying to figure out a way to get us out of here."

"Any luck?" Natalie asks him.

Chase shakes his head.

"Looks like we're still stuck for a bit," I say.

"At least one of us doesn't seem to mind," Natalie says. She gestures at Stitch beside me. The dog is sprawled out on a plush dog bed and still snoring away.

"We got to figure something out," Scout laments. "We need to get home."

"There's nothing to figure out," I say. "We just have to wait until they go away. However long it takes."

"They might never go away," Natalie says.

The thought hangs there for a moment. Even though I don't want to admit that it is a possibility, it really is a strong possibility.

Stitch finally shifts in the bed and then he twists his body and sits up and cocks his head to the side and stares at me. Then I realize what woke him up. He heard something. I listen closely to the sounds of the dead outside, but I hear something else, too.

"Shooting," I say.

"We can't shoot our way out of here," Chase sighs.

"No," I say. "Listen. I think someone is shooting."

CHAPTER FOURTEEN

It seems like the gunfire gets louder for a few minutes. Perhaps whoever is shooting is getting closer to our location.

"Sounds like there must be at least half a dozen automatic weapons firing to me," Chase says.

"Do you think they might be with us?" I say. "Maybe when they didn't hear from us they sent a team out after us."

"I don't think so," Chase says. "Some of those shots sound like they came from an AK."

"So who the hell would be crazy enough to be out here?" Scout says.

"Reapers," Chase says.

The gunshots seem more distant now, as though they're moving away from the area again. The dead aren't quite as loud now. They wander away from the door and shamble away in the direction of the battle. I can see there are just a few left outside now.

"Whoever they were, they just saved our asses," I say.

"Let's get the hell out of here," Scout says.

We grab our gear and get ready by the door. Even though only one or two corpses remain between the door and the vehicles, there are still hundreds of the dead in the parking lot and the nearby streets.

All I hear anymore is the moaning sound of the dead outside. The shooting has stopped. Whoever it was is probably either dead or is too far away for us to hear their gunfire anymore.

Chase and I pry open the sliding door together as quietly as we can. As soon as the gap is big enough, Stitch bolts out the door. Natalie steps through with Scout right behind her. They each use their rifle to knock down the pair of corpses near the doors, while Chase and I hop out and get in the passenger side of the trucks.

I climb across to get behind the wheel while Stitch jumps into the car behind me. The first corpses from the throng of them in the parking lot reach the Tahoes.

"Hurry up!" I urge Scout.

She gets in and shuts the door. The dead lunge at me smacking their skulls against the window as I start the car. I shift gears and hit the gas. Tires squeal and we peel out of the parking lot behind Chase.

The dead are everywhere. One after another they step in

front of the vehicles and then they disappear beneath the wheels of the Tahoes. The vehicle bounces so much going over the bodies that I hit my head on the roof a couple of times. I probably should have fastened my seatbelt but there wasn't time.

Chase takes a sharp left down the first cross street and then drives onto the sidewalk to avoid a pileup in the middle of the road. There isn't any room to maneuver on this block so he just accelerates to plow through the corpses. A couple of the bodies fly through the windows of the shops.

The road opens up again and Chase swerves back off the sidewalk. I keep as close as I can to his bumper to avoid running over as many of the dead as possible. After a couple more blocks, we seem to get clear of the worst of it. The road expands to four lanes and then we are able to slow down a little once again. I don't loosen my grip on the wheel until I see the sign for the highway up ahead.

"We made it," I say and breathe a sigh of relief.

Scout looks over at me and sees how happy I am, and then she smiles, too.

Even though we didn't all make it and this could have gone much better, the fact is, we actually did what we had to do. We found what we needed. Now we just need to get it back home. Then we can fix all this. We can find a way to stop the dead.

"I can hardly believe it," Scout says. I remember what

she said about having a bad feeling yesterday. She never thought we'd make it home alive. But here we are.

"We're gonna be okay," I tell her.

She turns and looks back at me, but the smile on her face falters. I'm not quite sure why. Maybe it was because we still lost someone. Scout always takes something like that the hardest of all of us.

"Another hour we'll have you back with Stevie," I say, hoping it will give her something more pleasant to think about it.

I can't really tell whether or not it even registers with her at all, though. She stares through the windshield at the road ahead of us. I reach down to my bag and unzip the top. My hand searches around inside until I locate a pair of glass bottles and remove them from the bag.

Scout watches me out of the corner of her eye and then shakes her head when I hold out the bottles.

"Take one," I tell her.

She lets out a long sigh, but takes one of the beers reluctantly and twists off the cap. I open mine as well then hold the bottle up.

"Cheers," I say.

She finally smiles a little and lifts her bottle and clinks the rim against mine.

"I suppose we earned this," she says before she holds the bottle to her lips and tips it back.

"Damn right we did," I say.

I take a long gulp myself while I keep an eye on the back

bumper of the truck in front of us. The warm beer tastes like it sat all summer in a hot building, which is exactly right, but it's something at least.

Scout looks at the bottle in her hands for a long moment, then she raises it up again.

"To Hawk," she says.

I raise my bottle and clink hers again and take another long swig. I try not to think too far ahead of getting back home, but I can't really help it.

I get lost in my thoughts. I think about the future.

Fixing all of this.

Rebuilding.

For the first time, I really believe a life that isn't full of misery is obtainable. After everything we've been through, we might finally have a refuge from the dead. We may even be able to start taking our country back.

The afternoon sun seems a little brighter than usual as it shines down on the mountains to the west. I take another swig of beer and roll down the window for Stitch. He pokes his head out and savors the cool breeze against his face.

For the first time that I can remember in a while, it feels good to be alive.

The feeling lasts until we drive up the frontage road to the military installation and I see the steel doors are wide open. The auto-turrets above the entrance do nothing while the dead shamble into the tunnel of Cheyenne Mountain Complex. The place is completely overrun.

"No," I say.

"Oh my god," Scout gasps.

Chase stops the truck in front of us. I hit the brakes as well and sit there staring at the tunnel for a long moment until Chase calls on the radio.

"We're going in," Chase says.

"Right behind you," I confirm.

Chase hits the gas and starts speeding toward the tunnel. I follow right behind him, pushing the engine as we smash through the countless corpses on the road.

The dead are everywhere.

All I can hope is that we find the blast doors are still sealed.

Scout has that look on her face again, and I finally understand what she was feeling before. My stomach feels like a damp towel that is being wrung out.

Something very bad has happened.

Now we have to go in and find out just how bad it is.

CHAPTER FIFTEEN

We enter the dark tunnel and plow through the dead on the narrow road. Dark blood splatters across the windshield and the engine of the Tahoe sputters. Both of these vehicles have taken about as much abuse as they can handle. I just hope they can get us down the tunnel.

After we pass through the open chainlink gate, the blast doors come into view. They are wide open, too. Devoured remains of dead soldiers lie in puddles of dark blood outside the door.

I hear gunfire inside the facility. They're still alive.

I grab my rifle and jump out of the Tahoe as the dead close in around us. The dead walking through the blast doors turn around and come after us. I take aim and fire to clear a path inside as we hustle toward the door.

I am vaguely aware of Stitch barking nearby, but as we

get inside I turn around to look and don't see the mutt anywhere. I'm not sure if he is still in the car or if the idiot ran the wrong way in the tunnel. Either way, I can't afford to worry about him right now. Stupid dog.

"Cover me," Chase yells as he runs to the control room to close the blast door.

We have no idea how many of the dead might be inside. I'm not really sure if we're better off to lock ourselves inside of here, but keeping the door open is only going to allow them to keep pouring inside. I guess we have no other choice but to close it if we have any hope of taking back the facility.

I lay down some fire on the corpses coming up from the tunnel. Scout and Natalie cover the hallways. The dead are all over inside, blood and carnage are everywhere. Chase gets the blast door going. The alarm that blares whenever the facility goes into button-up goes on, and Chase hustles back to help me hold off the horde while the door slowly inches closed.

Even though it only takes about ninety seconds, it feels like an eternity. Out of the corner of my eye, I can't help noticing the dead creeping toward us down the hall. It makes me anxious and a little unsteady as I try to aim at the corpses coming straight at me. I go through two full mags and am starting to get really concerned about how much ammo we have left.

Finally, the massive door closes and crushes the last pair of corpses trying to get through the breach. I pivot around and scan the hallways. Now that we secured the entrance, I'm not sure what we should do next, but what I want to do is find Danielle. I'm not even sure where to even begin looking. She could be in the clinic or back in our room. She could be anywhere.

"We need to get to the lab," Chase says. "The doctor and Claire."

"I have to find Stevie," Scout says and she takes a few steps down the hall to the right. "I'm sorry."

Chase watches her go down the hall. His jaw clenches and lips press together as he turns to look at me.

"We'll split up," he says and jerks his head toward Scout. "Got the radio?"

I hold it up as I backpedal toward the hall, then I turn and run after Scout. I catch up to her when she stops to shoot at a pair of corpses in weathered clothes. She squeezes the trigger and puts them each down with one shot then she pivots around the corner with her gun ready and takes out another corpse down the hall.

As long as I've known Scout, she has been able to handle a weapon well, but I've never seen her like this. She is like a killing machine right now.

I let her take the lead as we move down the hallway. We advance cautiously, but quickly. Some of the doorways in the hall are wide open. As we go by, I see a mutilated body on the floor. I debate firing a shot to make sure it stays down, but I really don't have bullets to spare.

More screams and gunshots can be heard through the

ventilation system. Then someone closer cries out. It sounds like it must be down another one of the hallways on this floor.

"No!" a woman screams. "No!"

Gunshots.

Then more silence.

We turn down another hallway on the right and Scout curses. I look to see about ten corpses wandering down the corridor. I whirl around to support Scout as she opens fire. I take out a man in a dress uniform and a woman in blood-smeared flannel pajamas.

Then I hear a scream behind me and I spin back around to check the way we come.

A heavy man in boxer shorts sprints down the adjoining hallway. A moment later, a trio of moaning corpses stumbles after him. Even though I have a shot at them, I hesitate to pull the trigger. They're not coming after us. So I just watch them go by us.

Maybe that was the wrong thing to do.

I spin back around and see Scout already moving ahead. We step over the bodies while Scout swaps in a full magazine. One of the things reaches up and grabs her boot. Even though she shot it through the eye, the dead man still tries to pull itself up to bite her.

I fire another round into his head and he collapses to the floor and releases her leg. Then she starts moving forward again through the long corridor toward the housing structure.

There are no more threats ahead of us for the moment, but the signs that they were here are everywhere. The floor is covered in bloody footprints and shell casings. Streaks of blood, bullet holes, and handprints mar the walls.

We turn down the hallway to our suites and Scout runs to the open door of her room. She stops at the threshold and I watch her as her eyes scan the room. She starts to shake her head and she takes a couple of steps backward.

"He's not here," Scout cries.

I open the door to my room and find it empty as well. No sign of Danielle. Then I walk down to the next door and open it up. Amanda screams and tries to hit me over the head with a lamp as soon as I step inside the room. I swat her arm away and grab ahold of her.

"It's me," I say and shake her gently.

Her fearful eyes stare at me.

"Where is everyone?" I ask her.

She just looks at me and starts to cry. I shake her harder.

"You must have seen something!" I snap. "What happened?"

Amanda lowers her eyes to the floor and I realize how pointless it is to ask her anything. She either doesn't know or she is too traumatized to say anything. More gunshots in the hall. I release my hold on Amanda and then turn to look at Scout. She lowers the rifle again and her eyes look from Amanda to me.

"She doesn't know anything," I tell Scout.

"We have to keep looking for them," Scout says.

"I'm with you," I say.

"Blake," the radio crackles to life as Chase transmits. "You there, Blake?"

I shoulder my rifle and reach for the radio. His voice sounds different. He sounds almost emotional.

Scout steps back out of the room and looks up and down the hall. She adjusts her grip on the rifle impatiently as she waits for me.

"I'm here," I respond.

"It's all over, man" he says. "Claire. The doc. They're both fucking dead."

Scout looks back over her shoulder at me. For a long moment, I just hold the radio as the words sink in. Everything we fought for up to now was all for nothing. Gone in the blink of an eye.

"Did you find the kid?" he asks me.

"Negative," I say. "We're still looking."

"I hate to say it," Chase says. "But we need to just get the fuck out of here before we all end up dead."

Scout shakes her head. I know there is no way she is leaving without Stevie. I am not about to give up on finding Danielle either.

"The tunnel is full of those things so we'll have to use one of the emergency tunnels," Chase continues. "Look for a large red hatch."

"We're going to keep looking," I tell him.

"Don't be fucking stupid, man," Chase says.

"Take Natalie and head out," I say. "We'll be behind you soon."

"Blake!" he yells. "Blake!"

"Let's get to the clinic," I say to Scout. I can't be sure that is where they are, but it is the next logical place I can think to look for them.

I stuff the radio in the pocket of my packet and grab Amanda by the arm. She drags her feet at first, but then reluctantly starts walking once we step out into the bloody hallway and she sees all carnage.

Scout leads us down the hall toward the staircase. She is no longer being as cautious as she should be. Every second we waste could be the difference between life and death for Stevie and Danielle.

We reach the door to the staircase with bloody fingerprints on the handle. Scout opens the door and then bloody hands latch on to her from the darkness. She fires blindly in the stairwell until the thing flops back on the floor.

Inside the stairwell, two more corpses wander on the landing below. I let go of Amanda for a moment and fire at them while Scout reloads another mag.

A corpse in fatigues collapses against the wall. I shift my aim to a man in sweat pants and a wife-beater and fire again. His head snaps back and then he tumbles down the stairs.

We hustle down both flights to the bottom floor. Over the echo of our feet on the concrete and the ringing in my ears, I still hear the muffled gunfire in other parts of the building. Cheyenne Mountain might be lost, but not without one hell of a fight.

In the hallway, another three corpses linger on the opposite side of the door. Scout opens the door and we go into the hall firing.

One of the men gets too close and I have to shove him back. It's harder than usual because these people just recently turned. They aren't as frail as the bony corpses we encounter out there. The man stumbles to the floor and then I raise the rifle and fire before he can get to his feet again.

"Come on," Scout says.

She is already running down the hall toward the medical lab. I grab Amanda by the arm again and start running after her. We round a corner and at the end of a long hallway, we enter another structure.

I notice the elevator to the safe room and wonder vaguely if the President might still be alive. Maybe I should stop. Maybe that is more important in the grand scheme of things. But finding Danielle is more important to me.

Then we hear gunfire close by. Someone cries out for help. At the next hall, Scout rounds the corner and then skids to a stop. The corridor is pack with at least twenty or thirty corpses. They are preoccupied with devouring the man that we just heard screaming a few moments ago. Now he is dead.

I freeze for a moment and look on in horror as the corpses tear into his dripping organs with their teeth. A couple of them notice us standing there and start shuffling down the hall after us. Scout whirls around and pushes me to go back. It takes me another second or two before I manage to peel my eyes off the nightmarish scene in the hall and get my legs working again, but then we turn and run back around the corner.

We don't have enough ammunition left to fight all of those things. We'll have to circle around the next hallway to get to the clinic. Amanda starts to drag her feet again. I glance back and she is looking ready to give up.

"I'm sorry," I pant. "But you have to keep going."

It doesn't seem to have much effect. We reach the next hallway and take a right turn once again. At the end of the corridor, I see the clinic. The broken glass windows and doors from yesterday are boarded up, so it's impossible to see if anyone is still inside.

Scout flings open the door and we rush inside the waiting area.

It's empty.

Scout turns around in a circle and he eyes search the room again.

"Stevie!" she calls out. "Stevie!"

She starts searching behind the desk and in the first exam room. I can tell she is about to lose it. If he were here and alive, he would have come out when he heard her.

Something crashes to the floor at the back of the clinic. I raise the rifle up and stare down the hall.

"Stevie?" Scout says.

A moan is the only response. Whatever is back there isn't Stevie. Not anymore.

I walk forward a few steps to get in front of Scout. At first, I just see a shadow on the floor as the figure shuffle from the back room. I ready the gun and prepare my nerves. The corpse moans again before it steps out into the hall.

The muzzle of the rifle dips toward the floor when I realize I am looking at Danielle. Her long dark hair hangs over her half-eaten face and her vacant eyes stare at me as she shuffles down the hall.

I shake my head in disbelief at the sight of her like this. A moment later, a bullet hits her in the forehead. Her body flops to the floor.

"Come on!" I hear Chase saying.

I slowly turn and find him standing behind me. Everything seems muffled and blurry and dulled all of a sudden.

"We have to get the fuck out of here!" Chase yells.

Natalie is standing behind him at the entrance. She holds the door open with her body as she fires as the dead coming down the hall.

"I still have to find Stevie," Scout insists.

"Forget it," Chase says. "He's gone."

"No," Scout says. "I'm going to find him."

She begins to walk away but Chase grabs her by the wrist. I just stand there staring at them in a daze. Then I glance back at Danielle on the floor. I still just can't believe it.

"Let go of me," she says.

"Sorry, Scout," Chase says. "I'll drag you out of here if I have to, but I'm not letting you go kill yourself."

"Hurry it up in there," Natalie yells between shots.

Chase lets go of Scout, and then he grabs my arm and shakes me violently.

"Snap the fuck out of it," Chase says to me. "We need to move."

"Okay," I mumble. I take one look back at Danielle on the floor and then I follow the others to the door.

CHAPTER SIXTEEN

There is no more gunfire in the depths of Cheyenne Mountain by the time we make our escape. We duck into the escape hatch and start climbing a ladder that seems to go on forever. No matter how much we pull ourselves up it seems like we're never closer to the speck of light above us.

Finally, we emerge into the moonlight on the side of the mountain. The night is cool and we watch the exhaled air coming out of our lungs as we try to catch our breath.

We have no vehicle, no food, and hardly any ammunition left. Even if we had any idea what our next move should be, we are just too devastated to go on right now. So we sit in the darkness and wait for daylight.

Scout and Amanda sit silently nearby me as I stare up at the countless stars in the sky. Natalie and Chase move a bit farther away and whisper quietly back and forth.

They're probably trying to figure out what to do. I don't even care right now.

Everything is gone. All that we fought for.

It doesn't just seem like the end of the world. It really is the end of the world.

Any hope we had of stopping the dead is gone forever. Now the only future I can envision appears even darker than the night sky. I've never felt such hopelessness before now.

I know Scout feels it, too. Even though I can't bring myself to look at anyone, I hear her quietly crying for hours. She can't seem to stop.

Chase returns to check on us and tells us to try and get some sleep.

"Me and Nat can take turns on watch," he adds.

None of us respond.

His presence did finally cause me to look around again. I notice Amanda sitting silently a few feet away and staring at nothing. To be honest, I'd forgotten she was even there. Maybe because she hardly is there anymore.

Not quite a person. More like an empty shell of a person.

I wonder if that is all that awaits me now.

All this time, I'd really just been ignoring the reality of our situation. I wanted to believe we had a chance. Even while I knew the odds were against us, I kept believing that for some reason we were outliers. That we were special for some reason because we were trying to stop all this from happening. Like we all had a role in some story that would keep going as long as it took for us to prevail.

But it was never going to happen. We were always destined for death.

It's just a matter of time now.

There is no more future. No rebuilding. No going back to our old lives.

The only refuge for us now is death.

Something stirs in the brush nearby. For some reason, I don't even bother to say something to warn anyone else.

A few seconds later, Chase stops whispering to Natalie and turns toward the sound. He raises his rifle and peers into the darkness.

Stitch emerges from the shadows and Chase lowers the rifle again.

The mutt wags his tail and walks over to me and sits down at my feet, pressing his body against my calf and stares up at me.

I put my hand on top of his head and scratch him gently. It isn't much but in some small way it helps right now in a small way to feel connected to something.

Stitch licks at my palm and then lets out a little whimper. He stares at the woods where he came from for a long time. Then I hear the moans and I understand. The dead are still coming for us.

Maybe the stupid dog led them up the mountain or some instinct brought them. Either way, they're here.

"We need to go," Chase says. "If we climb to higher

ground the rough terrain will keep them from following after us."

He stares at us for a few seconds. None of us make a move to get up. He turns his head and looks over at Natalie and shakes his head.

"I told you," he says.

Natalie walks over to me and crouches down in front of me. She puts her face right in front of mine to make eye contact with me.

"Blake," she whispers. "Get up. It's time to go."

Scout gets to her feet. She grabs her gear and gets ready to climb. Stich lets out a low growl as the scent of the dead nearby drifts over on the breeze.

"I know what you've been through," Natalie says. "And I know that you can do this. Don't quit now."

"Okay," I agree finally. It feels like it takes all my strength just to say the words.

"Good," Natalie says.

I get to my feet and grab my bag and look at Amanda. I feel like I understand her now.

"Come on," I say without expecting a response.

I grab her by the arm and help her to her feet and then we march up the mountain as the dead pursue us. We keep climbing higher and higher over the rocky terrain. Beneath the towering pines, we walk through the blackness, stumbling over rocks and listening to the haunting sound of the dead.

As the climb gets more difficult, we have to pause to

catch our breath in the thin mountain air. Each time we stop the dead sound farther behind us, slowed by the natural landscape.

Finally, our boots stop crunching through the snow when dawn approaches. The only thing we hear is the icy breeze and our heavy breathing.

I drop my pack and rifle in the snow and lean against a boulder and stare at the dying world far below us. We're safe for now up here, but there is no way to survive at this altitude indefinitely. Eventually, we will have to return.

"We're going to freeze to death up here," Scout says.

"You're not gonna freeze," Chase says. "Back when this all started I was doing mountain survival training with my unit."

He pauses for a long moment while he is lost in his memories.

"Seems like so long ago," he says. "We were up in a mountain like this for three weeks without much of anything. We can work our way around the mountain and head down on the other side."

"No," Scout shakes her head. "Stevie is still out there somewhere. I have to find him. He is all alone."

"Scout," Chase sighs. "I'm sorry. I liked the kid, too. But—"

"He's alive!" Scout yells. She presses a hand against her chest. "I can feel it."

Chase shakes his head, turns his back to her and stalks away staring at his footprints in the snow.

"That's bullshit, Scout," he says. "You know it as well as I do. There is no way he is still alive down there. I can't stop you from going to see that for yourself, but you can count me out of going back there. It's suicide."

"Scout," Natalie agrees. "I hate to say it, but Chase is right. We need to be realistic."

"I am being realistic," Scout cries. "He is just a kid and I am not just going to give up."

She marches away through the snow in the direction we came.

"Scout," Natalie calls after her.

"Just let it go," Chase says to Natalie. "She's not going anywhere right now."

I watch as Scout stops about thirty yards away. She folds her arms across her chest and stares at the world.

"What do we do now?" I say to no one in particular. I don't really expect an answer.

"We get the hell out of here as soon as possible," Chase says.

"Leave?" I say. The thought had not occurred to me because I have no idea where else we might go from here.

"Yeah," Chase says. "Face it, man. We lost. Everyone is dead. It's all over."

I look at Scout again. I know she won't leave here.

"There's nothing left for us here," Chase says. "The Reapers control everything around here. We should just get the hell out of here. Go as far as we can."

He might be right, but I don't know that I have it in me to go back on the road again.

"There's nothing left for us anywhere," I say.

"That may be so," he agrees. "But my mission here is done. I'm going home now. The rest of you can do whatever you want."

He turns around and grabs his pack and rifle off the ground. Natalie picks up her pack as well. Both of them watch me expectantly, but I don't make a move to get up.

"Last chance," Chase warns me.

I shake my head.

"You're making a big mistake," he says and then he marches away in the snow.

Natalie lingers behind a moment, then walks over and bends down and hugs me. It doesn't surprise me that she doesn't want to stay behind. Look at where following me got us. I'm worried for her that she wants to be so much like Chase, but I'm starting to understand it more. It's about survival for those two.

"I'm so grateful for everything," Natalie whispers to me.

"Take care of yourself," I say.

She stands back up and I can see the tears in her eyes.

"Let's go," Chase calls to her.

She sniffs and swipes at her wet cheeks with her sleeve.

"Goodbye, Blake," she says.

Then Natalie walks away, too. I watch them go until they disappear behind the snow. Scout slowly makes her way back toward me and Amanda. She stops a few feet away and looks at the tracks that Natalie and Chase left in the snow. It's not hard to see that she is really hurting inside.

"Do you think they will come back?" she asks.

"I wouldn't bet on it," I admit.

Scout starts to cry again.

"I'm sorry," she sobs. "I just can't leave without him."

As long as she can keep telling herself there is a chance he might be alive, then she has a reason to keep going. If she were to give up on finding Stevie, then she would probably just give up completely.

"I know," I tell her.

It's hard to believe just how drastically our situation changed over the last day. I remove the last of the food in my pack, a few energy bars I snagged from the pharmacy yesterday, and hand one to Scout. I hold one out for Amanda as well and she just stares at it.

"You need to eat," I tell her.

When she still doesn't move to take it, I open the wrapper up and grab her arm and place it in her palm. She takes it but just holds it while I unwrap my own bar and eat beside her.

Amanda seems even worse now that Lacey isn't around. She is pretty much unresponsive to anything.

"Eat," I encourage her again.

She stares at the bar in her own hand for several minutes before she finally brings it up to her lips and takes a small bite from the corner and chews it slowly.

The sun reflecting off the layer of snow helps to keep us warm as the morning turns to afternoon. I close my eyes and drift into a light sleep for a little while until an explosion wakes me up again. I open my eyes and notice a column of smoke in the sky. It looks to be from the area near the entrance to Cheyenne Mountain.

CHAPTER SEVENTEEN

"We need to go back," Scout says.

"I don't think that's a good idea yet," I say.

"All the dead will be headed for the explosion," she says.

I shake my head. I'm not sure I can handle much more right now.

"We can't hide up here forever," she says and waves her hands around wildly to show her frustration.

When I don't respond, she picks up her pack and slings it over her shoulders and then grabs her rifle.

"I guess I'll go by myself then," she says.

"Okay," I finally relent. "I'll come with you."

I gather my gear and we head back down the mountain toward the sound of small arms fire.

"Some of them must still be alive," Scout says bounding recklessly down the mountain.

I know Scout hopes that some of them survived, but I don't necessarily believe that is the reason for the small arms fire. I'm too out of breath to speak so I just keep it to myself.

I doubt it would do any good anyway.

Scout is the kind of person that won't believe something she doesn't want to unless she can see it for herself.

"Slow down," is all I can manage to say. I carry my rifle in one hand and use the other to help Amanda down the tricky terrain.

Scout just keeps going as fast as she can. Stitch trots ahead of her, pausing every couple hundred yards when he gets too far in front of us. His nose sniffs the air and then he decides it safe to keep going.

"We're getting close," Scout says as the gunfire gets louder. "Hurry up."

Some of the weapons are not rifles. It sounds like there are at least a couple of fifty-caliber machine guns. A couple of months ago, I'd never know the difference, but these are the things I've had to learn in order to survive.

"Scout!" I plead. "Stop!"

She freezes and looks around. My desperate tone alarmed her.

"What is it?" she asks.

"Listen," I say. "I don't think those guns are ours."

Scout looks confused for a moment as if I am not making any sense.

"Just listen," I say.

She tilts her head slightly to listen and then the creases in her brow vanish as she realizes what I'm talking about.

"Reapers," she says. "What are they doing here?"

"I don't know. We can't just go running in there, though," I pant when I catch up to her and turn to help Amanda climb down the jagged rocks.

All of a sudden, a flip seems to switch and when Scout looks at me I can see she is thinking rationally and focused once again.

"Okay," Scout says. "We'll just get close enough to see what's happening."

"Good," I agree.

We get down to the escape hatch that we climbed out of last night. The landing overlooks the main entrance to the base. Scout pulls out a pair of binoculars from her bag and recons the scene below. Then she hands the binoculars to me.

"It's them," she says.

I take a look for myself and can hardly believe my eyes.

"Oh my god," I whisper.

"There's a lot of them," Scout says.

Until now we had never encountered more than a couple of the Reaper narco tanks at one time. We knew there must be a lot of them, but I never imagined the kind of army that was before us. There had to be more than fifty fighting vehicles with improvised armor. Some of them giant RV's. They even have a couple of tanks. And those were just the ones we could see. They had to have people that are already inside the mountain as well.

"Looks like they're taking it over," I say.

Then I notice a group of people in uniform. It's hard to tell from this distance, but they don't look to be with the Reapers. Maybe there were some survivors that had been captured.

"Looks like they found some survivors," I inform Scout.

"Where?" she says and snatches the binoculars from my hands.

I point to show her the general location and wait while she scans the area.

"I can't see from here," Scout complains. "I'm going closer."

"That's a bad idea," I say, but I know there is no stopping her now.

"They'll never know we're here," Scout says. "Trust me."

She leads us down the mountainside toward bluff a few hundred yards from the entrance. By now, most of the area surrounding the facility has been cleared of the dead. Scout scans the area with her binoculars again and locates the survivors.

"Looks like they have McGrath," Scout says. "They've got them tied up."

She adjusts the knob and squints.

"No sign of Stevie," she adds and shifts the binoculars slightly. "Wait a minute..."

I wait expectantly for her to go on. I can't help but hope that maybe she will find Stevie alive after all.

"Son of a bitch," she curses.

"What?" I say.

She shoves the binoculars toward me.

"Look near the RV," she says.

I bring the binoculars to my eyes and scope the area. I'm not even sure what I am supposed to be looking for.

"Do you see him?"

I don't see any kids in sight, but then I see who she is talking about.

"That's Andrew," I say.

"Motherfucker," Scout seethes.

I watch a moment longer. One of the Reapers approaches Andrew and he stops the man and points a finger and then the man nods and hustles away. He isn't just one of them, he is ordering them around.

The pieces start to come together immediately. This outbreak was not just because of some bacterial infection in the facility. The Reapers let the dead inside. They planned all of this. They murdered Danielle. And the worst part is, it was me and Scout that took them in.

My blood feels like it's suddenly boiling beneath my skin.

"I'm going to fucking shoot him," Scout says as she

props her rifle upon the rock and presses her eye to the scope.

"You'll never hit him from here," I say and cover the lens with my hand.

She pulls her head back and grits her teeth together. Scout may not like it, but she knows I'm right. She pulls the rifle back down and twists herself around so that her back leans against the rock. I don't know if she has just seen enough, or if that is the only way she feels like she can resist the urge to try and take a shot at Andrew.

I keep watching him move around for a few more minutes. He gestures at the prisoners and then some of the Reapers pick them up and bring them to an open patch of road that is encircled by vehicles.

It looks like they have about fifteen men and women along with McGrath. One appears to be with his secret service security detail. About half the others are in uniforms, and the others look to be civilian contractors. The Reapers force them to line up on their knees. The prisoners sit there for several minutes while the Reapers lean against their vehicles. Finally, they drag one more woman over with the others. It takes a minute before I recognize her.

"I see Lacey," I say.

I pull down the binoculars and glance at Amanda. Her eyes are suddenly very alert and she looks at me.

"Do you want to see?" I ask her.

Without a word, Amanda takes the binoculars from my

hands. I sense what is about to happen, and I have no desire to see it. Neither does Amanda. She passes the binoculars back to me and I can see the tears streaming down her cheeks. I can't help but wonder if she'd still react that way if it was me down there instead of Lacey. I'm not so sure anymore.

Andrew walks down the row of hostages. He takes his time as he fires a bullet in the back of their heads. I lower my eyes to avoid seeing it, but I still hear the shots. When it's finally over, I look down and see the bodies sprawled on the ground, their faces resting in puddles of blood.

As horrible as it was to see this, I know there is nothing that we could have done to stop it. We're alone with a handful of bullets between us. If we had intervened we'd just end up dead, too.

"Let's get out of here," I say. Suddenly, I regret that we didn't leave with Chase. There is nothing left for us here.

We pick ourselves up off the ground and retreat into the woods. It's already the middle of the afternoon and we have no idea where we're going. The only thing I know for sure is that I never want to witness anything like what just happened ever again.

CHAPTER EIGHTEEN

The engine sputters when Scout turns the key.

"Try giving it some gas or something," I say.

She cranks it again but the truck just whirs and coughs and dies again.

"Maybe it's the spark plugs," I guess. I really have no idea what I'm talking about, though. Cars are not my thing.

"It's not the spark plugs," Scout says. "It's probably the gas."

"It says it's got half a tank," I point out.

"Yeah, I know it has gas," Scout rolls her eyes. "I mean the gas is probably stale."

We spent all night walking through the mountains. Since Cheyenne Mountain was a completely restricted zone before the collapse, we had to walk a long way before we found shelter. The small log cabin in the mountain smelled of urine and mouse shit. After the owner died or left, the wildlife in the area obviously clearly claimed this place as their own.

Mice nibble on crumbs on the countertop. There are several bird nests in the rafters and globs of white shit all over the floor. The dry goods in the cupboard have all been eaten by rodents. They even chewed through the aluminum cans somehow.

The best thing about this place is that there was a truck in the driveway. If only we could get it to start.

Scout opens up the back of the truck and searches around in the bed. She sighs and closes the rear gate again and looks around. Then she spots a dilapidated shed and I follow her as she marches over to it.

"I didn't even know gas went bad," I admit.

"What kind of man were you?" Scout wonders.

She opens the door of the shed and scans the shelves full of paint cans and bottles. Then she spots one and wipes the layer of dust from the label.

"What's that?" I ask.

"Hopefully this is the shit that will start the car," Scout says as she closes the shed again and heads back to the truck. "If there is any water from condensation in the tank, this should help to absorb it."

I glance over to make sure that Amanda is still okay on the front steps outside the house. She sits there on the steps with her head leaning against the railing post and her eyes closed.

Scout flips open the gas cover and then she twists off the cap. She pours the contents of the bottle into the gas tank. When it's empty she just tosses the plastic bottle on the ground. There was a time when watching someone do that would have bothered me. Worrying about the environment is kind of pointless now anyway, I guess. It's just a matter of time before we're all dead.

"Going to have to give it a few minutes," Scout says and leans back against the chassis of the truck. She folds her arms across her chest and stares at the woods around us.

I lean against the truck next to her and watch Stitch amusing himself by picking up a stick with his jaws and swinging it around until he settles down and gets to work chewing on one end of it. A chill causes me to shiver and tuck my hands into the pockets of my jeans. It seems like I should say something to her about Stevie, but I don't know what to say and I don't want to make her feel worse than she already does.

"You really meant the world to her," Scout says to me. "Danielle, I mean."

I turn my head to look at her. Scout glances over at Amanda and then looks me in the eyes again.

"She wasn't upset about Amanda at all," Scout says. "She wasn't like that. I can't say I'd have had the same reaction if I were in her place, but not Danielle."

It makes me smile to hear her say it.

"Not Danielle," I agree. "She wasn't like that."

"She just wanted you to be happy, Blake," Scout says.

"So if you cared about Danielle at all, don't give up on it now. Even if happiness might seem impossible, keep trying to figure it out. That's what Danielle would have wanted for you."

I nod my head and then look down at the ground. Then it all starts to really hit me. My face tightens and the tears blur my eyes. I cover my face with my hand and just let it out. Scout puts an arm around me and waits for it to pass.

"Thanks, Scout," I finally manage to say.

"Let's get this thing started and get out of this dump," she says.

"Agreed," I say.

"I've been thinking," Scout says. "Remember that ranch we found."

"Of course, I remember it," I say.

"It's worth checking to see if it's still there," Scout says.

"We don't have anywhere else to go," I agree.

She climbs back in behind the wheel and turns the key and the truck sputters for several seconds before it coughs to life. The engine catches and Scout gives it some gas to keep it from dying. It revs and sputters some more but continues idling roughly.

"I think we're good," Scout says. "Just going to let it idle for a minute."

The noisy truck woke Amanda up from her nap and I wave for her to come over and get into the truck. I start to climb into the passenger side, but before I even open the door Scout stops me.

"Hey," she says. "I got it started. You can drive."

Scout gets back out and opens the back door and shoves some papers onto the floor so she can stretch out on the seat. I let Amanda into the passenger seat and close the door for her, then I get behind the wheel.

I shift the truck into gear and steer us slowly down the dirt road covered in fallen branches. They crack, break and then we leave the destroyed remains behind us forever.

We just move on.

Scout is already asleep in the backseat before we reach the highway. In the rearview mirror, I see her head resting on her pack and her mouth hanging open as she snores lightly. I glance over at Amanda in the passenger seat. She stares out the window at the world going by us.

I know that Scout probably did not take the whole back-seat just because she was tired. She usually sleeps just fine in the front seat. So I'm pretty sure she was just trying to get me and Amanda a chance to talk up in the front. I don't even know where to begin, though.

"I'm sorry about Lacey," I say.

Amanda doesn't seem to hear me at first. I'm about to say it again when she slowly turns her head and looks at me.

"I know you cared about her," I go on.

The corner of her mouth twitches slightly in what might have been nothing or could have been the briefest flicker of an appreciative smile. Before I figure it out she turns her head again and stares out the window.

It's not much, but maybe it's a start.

Amanda tilts her head back and sleeps as well as the long afternoon comes to an end. I return my focus to the road and trying to remember the way to the ranch. Without a map or GPS, I'm really just heading south until I spot something that looks vaguely familiar.

At least there is little chance of running into any of the Reaper patrols on the road right now since there were so many of them at Cheyenne Mountain.

I still can't believe that we couldn't see through Andrew. Usually, we were pretty suspicious of the people we came across. It just seemed like we could trust him after he helped save us. After Shawn lost his life trying to help Lana.

It still just blows my mind to think about it.

We let them right in and now the world is going to end and there is nothing that any of us can do to try and stop it.

It makes me wonder if there is any point in trying to survive anymore. What is there left to live for in this world?

I come to a road that looks familiar, but there aren't any signs. It heads south, but beyond that, I'm not entirely sure it is the same road we took when we drove up here from New Mexico. My eyes scan the vacant buildings as I bring the truck to a stop, but I still can't decide if this is the right way to go or not.

"Fuck it," I finally mutter under my breath. I make the turn down the unknown road anyway.

I'm already lost.

What does one more wrong turn matter anymore?

I keep driving south until I see a sign that indicates I am crossing into New Mexico once again. The gas light comes on and the truck dings periodically to remind me we are almost out of gas. About fifteen minutes later, we reach the familiar tiny town of Questa. A lonely corpse wanders out in front of the handful of small buildings.

A few miles down the road, I see the ranch. It still looks like it did the last time I was here. As the sun sets behind the mountains, I pull the truck into the long driveway and roll cautiously up to the house. The old shuttle bus that Fletcher lost his life trying to get still sits in the dusty driveway.

"We're here," I say.

Scout and Amanda stir from sleep and look around at the farm. I open the door and step out of the truck. While Scout stares at the shuttle bus, I grab my rifle and then take a look at the barns and the guest house. Everything seems like I remember, but it's hard to be exactly sure. There's always the chance that someone could be here.

When Scout is ready, I walk up the porch quietly and peer inside the thin windows beside the door. The inside of the house is dark. My hand turns the knob and then the sensor switches on the light as soon I the door opens. I step into the foyer, the rifle pointing around the adjoining rooms as I scan them. Everything is just as it was.

I lower the rifle and look at Scout. Stitch sniffs at the air and wags his tail, then he trots up the stairs and disappears into the master bedroom.

"I think it's safe to say no one was here," I say.

Scout nods as well and lowers her weapon. I walk back to the door and close it and flip the lock. Scout leaves the room and walks to the kitchen and a moment later I hear her digging around in the pantry.

Amanda looks around the house. She still seems concerned but also in awe of the place like we were when we first arrived here almost two months ago.

"Don't worry," I tell Amanda. "We'll be safe here."

Reluctantly she lets me lead her into the kitchen and takes a seat at the long kitchen table.

"We're home," I say softly. My tone isn't exactly sincere, but not quite sarcastic either. More like I'm stating a reality that we have to accept.

CHAPTER NINETEEN

I wake up in the morning in the bed next to Stitch. The beams of sunlight coming through the window cover the room in bars of shadow and light. For a long time, I just drift in and out of sleep and listen to the peaceful silence of the house and the occasional hum of the fan on the furnace blowing air through the vents.

Finally, I drag myself out of bed when my stomach growls to be fed. I head out of the room and start down the stairs, that's when I hear something in one of the other bedrooms. It sounds like crying. The noise stops suddenly and for a few seconds, I'm not sure if I actually heard it or if it was just my imagination.

I turn around and walk down the hall and stop at each door to listen.

As soon as I conclude that I must be going crazy and

turn to go back downstairs, I hear the crying again at the end of the hall. I walk over to the door and open it a few inches and see Amanda crying on the bed. When she notices me she stops crying and quickly wipes away the tears on her cheeks.

"Hey," I say. I suddenly feel bad for not knocking. "Are you alright?"

She doesn't say anything and just stares at me for a painfully long moment before she finally nods her head slightly. I wonder what is making her cry. It could be losing her friend yesterday. Maybe it was what I said to her before we left for Denver. I really can't be sure, but it feels like it is my fault.

"I know I said some things before," I start to say, but then I catch myself. This probably isn't the time. "Maybe it was wrong. I didn't mean to hurt you."

Her eyes stare up at me but she says nothing. I suddenly feel guilty. She has every right to hate me, I guess. I just wish she would say something.

"I'm here," I say. "If you ever want to talk."

Then I close the door and go back downstairs to let Stitch outside. When I turn down the hallway toward the kitchen, I find Scout is awake already and sitting in front of a full cup of coffee while she stares at nothing. She doesn't even react to me and Stitch as we enter the room.

"Good morning," I say.

The sound of my voice startles her so much that she inhales sharply and jumps in her seat before she looks over to see me in the hallway. Her shoulders relax and she smiles. Usually, Scout is way too alert to be caught off guard like that. She must have really been deep in thought.

"Didn't mean to startle you," I say.

"It's okay," she says. Her tired eyes turn away and she scrunches up her face when she looks at the coffee on the table in front of her, as though she isn't sure how it got there.

Stitch walks over to the patio door and looks outside at the wet grass in the backyard. He sits and pants impatiently until I come over and unlock the door and slide it open. He dashes out into the yard and runs circles around the property. At least one of us is excited to be back here.

I walk into the kitchen and open the cupboard and remove a coffee mug and pour myself a cup of the steaming pot on the counter. Then I walk back over and sit next to Scout. She is still staring at nothing and seems completely lost in her thoughts.

The coffee burns my lip when I try to take a sip, so I set it back down and listen to the silence in the room as I wait for it to cool. I feel the urge to say something, but I also don't feel like it either. I have plenty on my mind still as well. Part of the reason I didn't feel like getting up this morning was that when I was asleep it meant that I didn't have to think about everything that happened these last few days.

"I still can't even believe it," Scout says suddenly.

I think about it for a few seconds but I'm not exactly sure what she is talking about.

"What?" I say.

"This," Scout says. "All of it. Everything that happened to me since this whole thing started."

She stops again and continues to stare at the empty seat across the table.

"It's kind of hard to comprehend," I agree.

"I see all of them still," Scout says. "All their faces. So many of them."

My eyes move to the empty space across the table for a second and then I look at Scout again. I wonder who she is seeing there right now.

"It's really all over now," she says. Her throat tightens around the last sentence and her lower lip quivers slightly.

The thought occurs to me that Scout needs me to lie to her right now. She wants me to give her something positive to cling to. Some kind of a reason to go on.

To hope.

But I can't.

"Yeah," I agree. "I guess it is."

Scout doesn't even blink. Her eyes stay transfixed on the chair across from her. A wallclock over the kitchen table counts off the seconds as we sit and I can feel each fragment of time bringing us closer to our inevitable demise.

"I keep thinking how unfair it is," Scout says. "If I was

there I could have done something. I could have saved them."

"Hey," I say. "No. You can't blame yourself."

I realize the guilt she feels is just part of the progression of grief. She is working her way through the loss. To be honest, I'm still not even over the shock of what happened. I keep expecting Danielle to walk into the room again at any moment.

"Good morning."

The voice startles me and I turn and find Amanda standing there. Her eyes are still red from crying earlier, but she actually said something. I get up from my chair and gawk at her for a minute with my mouth hanging open as she enters the kitchen.

"Good morning," I finally manage to speak.

She folds her arms and her eyes look around the kitchen as she avoids my gaze.

"You want some coffee?" I ask her.

She averts her gaze from mine but nods her head.

"Sit down," I urge her. "I'll get you some."

Amanda sits down at the table across from Scout while I retrieve another mug from the cupboard and fill it up. I locate the sugar in a small container and pour a couple of spoonfuls in and stir. The metal spoon clinks loudly against the porcelain. The whole time I am standing at the counter I'm trying to comprehend that Amanda just spoke to me normally for the first time. It was just two words, but it still feels like something has suddenly shifted even if I have no idea what that could be.

I carry the cup over and set it down in front of her.

"Thanks, Blake," Amanda says. She picks up the cup and takes a sip.

"No problem," I say.

Then she presses her lips together and lowers her eyes.

For the briefest moment, it feels like talking to the woman I married again. Just as fast she resumes avoiding eye contact with me. Stitch barks once outside. I look at the window even though he is nowhere in sight. A second later he starts barking again.

"Idiot is going to bring every walking stiff for miles," I grumble.

"I'm going to see what he is up to," Scout says. She slides back her chair and gets up, reaching for the strap of her rifle slung over the seatback.

"Hang on. Let me give you a hand," I say and push my chair away from the table.

"It's alright," she says. "I'll be fine."

"I think it's better if we—"

"I can handle it," Scout interrupts me in the middle of my sentence. She slides open the door and gives me a hard look. I settle back into my chair.

For whatever reason, it's clear Scout would rather be alone right now. It makes me a bit anxious after talking with her, but it's not like I can stop her.

The door opens and Stitch starts barking even louder

and getting higher in pitch like he does when he gets really excited. Scout steps out onto the patio and turns around to shut the door.

"Be careful," I tell her.

"You worry too much," she tells me and then she slides the door closed and walks off.

Maybe Scout just wants to be alone, but I get the sense that she wanted me to keep talking to Amanda again. I pull my chair back in and pick up my coffee and take a sip, but I can't really think of what to say to her. I still have no idea how she feels. I wouldn't blame her if she hates me.

Before I make up my mind, a rifle report outside shatters the silent morning. Amanda jumps in her seat. Another shot echoes through the mountains a moment later.

Several minutes pass while I sit at the table in silence with Amanda and wait for Scout to return. It feels more awkward the longer we sit there and then I start wondering if Scout would consider doing something drastic.

Maybe she wanted to be alone out there for a different reason. Finally, I can't take it anymore. I slide my chair back and stand up.

"I'm going to go make sure she is okay," I say to Amanda.

She just watches me walking slowly toward the patio door. I peer through the glass but there is no sign of Scout or Stitch. Just a chilly silence as I stare at the glistening dew on the grass. I slide the door open and step onto the deck and look around.

"I'll be right back," I tell Amanda. Her eyes seem to glaze over again. I smile but she just stares at me while I close the door.

I'd be lying to say I'm not scared about what I might find out here, especially after seeing how Scout was acting this morning. I know she is a strong person, but at some point, it's hard not to look around right now and wonder what the point is anymore.

A chill runs down my spine while I stand on the deck and scan the property for any sign of Scout or Stitch. Birds call in the pine trees at the back of the property. I take a breath and notice the stench of rot in the air. When I look over to the left, I see the remains of the owners in front of the other patio door to the family room. The bodies have been devoured by wild animals. Maybe it was the living dead.

I walk down the stairs of the deck and step through the overgrown grasses. The green blades swish against my legs. I ready the rifle and head around the side of the house.

Then I see Scout sitting on the ground in the shade of a tree. Her back is to me and Stitch sits beside her. He notices me approaching them and trots towards me, his tail wagging.

Scout doesn't move. Her attention is focused on something on the ground in front of her.

"Scout," I say. "Are you okay?"

She doesn't answer, but as I get a few steps closer I become aware of what she is looking at. One the ground a few feet away from her is a crudely constructed wooden cross. The name Michael is scrawled in block letters on it. I take a few steps closer and see a small hand protruding from the ground. Brown dirt is embedded beneath the overgrown nails.

"Jesus," I whisper.

I lower the rifle when I reach Scout. She stares down at the lifeless face of a young kid, still mostly buried in the ground. The gun is still clenched in her hand and tears stream down her cheeks. I shoulder my weapon and reach down to grab her by the arm and pull her up.

"Come on, Scout," I whisper.

At first, her body is like dead weight when I try to help her to her feet. I pull harder until she finally begins to move and then I wrap my arm around her.

"It's okay," I whisper over and over to try to help her calm down but she just keeps crying. "Shhh. It's okay."

But that couldn't be further from the truth. We are not okay at all.

CHAPTER TWENTY

It all makes a little more sense now. The last time we were here we found the owners in the family room. None of us could figure out why someone would go through all the trouble of prepping for the apocalypse only to check out when the end of the world happened.

We never saw the grave that they dug outside.

Scout walks inside the house in a daze and then leaves the kitchen without a word. I get a metallic taste in my mouth and lean against the counter near the sink in case I feel sick. A door closes upstairs and a few minutes later the sound of water running.

"What happened?" Amanda finally asks. I'm surprised to find her watching me closely again. Even after every-thing, she finally seems to be opening up again. Maybe it's because she has no one else now that Lacey is gone. It could have something to do with me and Danielle. I have no idea, but I take it as a good sign.

"You probably don't want to know," I say. "It's okay, though. We're safe."

I turn on the faucet and grab a cup from the cabinet and fill it up. I gulp down the water to clear the taste from my mouth. Then I set the glass down and return to the table.

I take a seat across from Amanda and let out a long sigh that might make me seem irritated. Amanda fidgets with the handle of her coffee cup.

"Sorry," I say. My eyes close and I swipe my hand over my face and rub my eyes with my thumb and index finger. When I open my eyes again, the world still looks just the same. "I'm just still a little off, I guess."

I look over at her and she just stares at her fingers running over the handle of the cup. Maybe she is slipping back into whatever sort of trance she had been in the last few weeks. I let my hand fall to my lap and lower my eyes to the floor.

"She seemed very kind," Amanda says softly. "Danielle."

I lift my head again and look at her.

"She was," I say. "After I found Abby and thought you were gone, I nearly gave up. If it wasn't for Danielle I wouldn't be alive right now."

The final words catch in my throat and sound strange when I say them. I cover my mouth with my hand as if to get it under control.

Amanda looks at me. I can see the tears in her eyes that want to come out.

"I'm sorry," I shake my head. "I know you probably don't want to hear about this."

I feel guilty again. I look down at the ring on my finger. Even though I kept it on, I didn't stay faithful.

"You know," Amanda says. "You don't have to explain it to me. I understand. I thought you were dead, too."

I raise my eyes to meet hers. Then I can see what she is getting at. My eyes move down to see her thin fingers of her left-hand grazing the handle of the mug. When she notices me looking she stops fidgeting and covers her bare left hand with her right and then places them in her lap.

"When we left Chicago," she says. "I had nothing. Lacey kept us safe. But eventually, we ran out of gas. Then we ran out of food. And eventually, we got really desperate. So we had to use the only thing we had left of value to anyone."

I lower my face into my palm to avoid what I knew to be true but had not yet had to face until now. Danielle had told me there were some signs of sexual abuse when Amanda arrived. It bothered me, but I wasn't going to push her to talk about it.

"A couple of them were actually kind to me," Amanda goes on. "They looked out for us. At least until they got infected or someone killed them. But mostly they were bad, I think. I can't even remember one of their names."

She stops for a few seconds and looks up at the ceiling like she might find the names written up there.

"No, I've forgotten them all," she laughs even though her eyes are tearing up. "Lacey would give me pills to make it easier, and it was, but I think I lost track of them. They're all just a blur now."

Amanda sniffs and wipes beneath her eyes with her fingers.

"Lacey got so mad at me the first few times," Amanda says. "I remember that much. She said if she were as pretty as me, she would do it herself, and that I was being a drama queen about it. Then I figured out I just had to accept the fact that you were probably dead. That way I could stop being in love. I think that made it more bearable. But now I'm not sure I can ever flip the switch back on again."

As much as I wish she would stop, I feel like maybe she needs to say this out loud in order to come to terms with it. So I listen in agony and wish for the story to end.

Somehow it all still feels like my fault. If I had found her, she would have never gone through any of that.

"I'm so sorry," I tell her. "None of that should have ever happened."

Amanda scrunches her nose and squints at me.

"No," Amanda says. "You don't see. It had to happen like that. Otherwise, I would have probably died a long time ago."

The thought makes me pause and think for a moment.

"I don't regret any of it," Amanda says. "And you shouldn't either. This is just the world we live in now."

"So why now?" I ask her. "Why did you wait to tell me this until now?"

Amanda chews on her lip for a moment while she stares at me. I recognize the old habit from our many years together. It means she is about to lie to me.

"I was scared," Amanda says. "I didn't want you to know."

She looks away from me and stares out the patio door into the sunlight. I study her for a long moment, but then decide to let it go. She's been through enough. If that wasn't the reason, it might just be that she was mad and doesn't want to admit it now.

"So what now?" I finally ask.

"I don't know," Amanda says vacantly, still staring outside. "But I'm sure whatever comes next will happen soon enough."

Another chill runs down my spine. Amanda used to be such a caring person, now she is just cold and a little creepy.

"Things always keep happening until you stop breathing," she mumbles.

Then she starts humming some lullaby softly.

I get up from the chair and walk away from the table. I'm not sure where I'm going, but I feel like I need to get out of the room. Coming face to face with Amanda finally has been more than I can handle.

I head downstairs and find Scout sitting at the bar. I

grab a bottle from the counter and pour it into a tumbler and drink it without even glancing at the label.

Whiskey.

It burns my insides, but I refill the glass again and gulp it down again.

My stomach churns. I'm pretty sure it's not even from the whiskey as much as it was from hearing everything that Amanda went through. I can understand why she is so unstable now.

"I'm not so sure I can do this anymore," Scout says.

"Me either," I agree.

"I just want it to be over," she says and lifts her drink up and takes a small sip.

I refill my glass again and knock down the rising feeling of guilt with another burning shot of whiskey. It doesn't take long before everything gets a little blurry around the edges. The pain dulls. And after I take another drink, I'm not thinking about much of anything any longer.

Scout takes the bottle in front of me and my glass and pours another glass out for herself. She replaces the cap and puts the bottle on the other side of the bar before taking a sip from the glass.

Scout sits there silently for several minutes and finishes her drink before she sets the empty glass down on the counter. She places her hand on my shoulder for a moment and taps softly with her fingertips.

"You shouldn't drink so much," she says. "I've seen what it does to people."

Then she removes her hand from my shoulder and walks upstairs. I get up from the stool and the bad taste in my mouth returns. I walk into the bathroom, flick on the lights, and run the faucet. With a cupped hand, I splash cold water on my face, but it doesn't help.

My stomach gurgles and then I gag and barely keep the vomit in my mouth long enough to bend over the toilet. Moments later, my stomach is empty. Spittle drips from my lips and I swipe it away with the back of my hand.

I flush the toilet and clean up. My mind already feels relatively clear again now that the alcohol it out of my system. For a long time, I lean against the sink and stare at my face in the mirror and try to recognize the person I see there.

It's not just the fact that I am leaner now or have a lot more scars than I did before. I just don't know who I am anymore and I'm not sure that we'll ever be able to figure out who any of us are ever again.

CHAPTER TWENTY-ONE

Stitch wakes me up early in the morning. He lets out a concerned growl and stands up on the bed. Then he hops down to the floor and dashes into the hall.

I sit up in bed and listen for a moment. I hear someone fumbling around downstairs, but since Stitch isn't barking it probably is not trouble. After I grab my shirt off the bedpost and pull it on, I make my way to the hall. I follow the sound down the stairs and pause as I turn on the landing and find Scout loading up her pack in the foyer.

"What's going on?" I ask her.

She stops moving and looks up suddenly with her mouth hanging open.

"I'm leaving," she says.

"Seems more like you're sneaking out," I say.

"I'll be back," Scout assures me as she grabs a box of

protein bars off the storage bench and shoves them in her backpack.

"Where are you going?" I ask her.

Scout zips her pack closed and lets out a long sigh.

"I'm pretty sure you don't want to know," Scout says.

"What are you doing?" I ask again.

"I can't just let it go," Scout says.

"What are you talking about?" I keep moving down the stairs.

"I'm going after them," Scout says.

"After who?" I say, even though I know what she is getting at. I can't believe it unless I hear her say it out loud.

"You know who I'm talking about," Scout says. She grabs the strap of her pack and picks it up off the bench.

"Scout," I say. "You can't be serious."

"Look at me," Scout scoffs. "Of course, I'm serious."

She puts her other arm through the pack and shrugs it over her shoulder as she turns toward the door. I grab her arm and keep her from leaving.

"Scout," I tell her. "I'm not just going to let you leave by yourself."

"I don't care if I die," Scout finally says. "But I can't just accept what happened. They have to pay for what they did to us."

"Listen," I say, but Scout lowers her eyes and shakes her head as she breaks free from my grip. I can tell by her clenched jaw and focused stare that she has already made up her mind. There is no way I'm going to talk her out of this if that was my intention, but it isn't.

"There is nothing you can stay to stop me, Blake," she warns me.

"I know," I say. "I'm not going to try stopping you. I'm coming with."

"What?" Scout says. "What about Amanda?"

After yesterday, the thought of being alone here with Amanda frightens me as much as anything.

"She'll be safe here," I say.

"You don't have to do this," Scout says.

"I know. Give me five minutes to get ready," I say. "I'll meet you in the car."

I get dressed and load up on enough supplies and ammo for a couple of days and then I wake Amanda up with a knock on the door as the sun peeks over the horizon.

"I am leaving with Scout," I say.

Amanda sits up in the bed and rubs her eyes.

"Is something wrong?" she asks.

"Everything is fine," I assure her. "You'll be safe here until we get back."

"Where are you going?" she asks.

I don't want her to worry so I make up a lie. Even if there is a good chance Scout and I won't survive this, I don't need to make it any harder on Amanda.

"Supply run," I smile. "Winter is coming soon. We'll need to stock up as much as we can before then."

Amanda squints her tired eyes at me.

"Okay," Amanda finally says. I see her flop back down in the bed as I close the door.

Stitch follows me through the front door and then trots around me to get to the Tesla that belonged to the previous owners of the ranch. Scout sits behind the wheel and stares at the road while the car idles in the driveway. I open up the back door and let the dog hop onto the leather seats before I go around the vehicle to get in on the passenger side.

Scout looks over at me as I settle my pack on the floor below my legs. As soon, I nod she heads down the long driveway toward the highway.

"Any idea where we're going?" I ask her.

"Not a clue," Scout says.

She turns right and we head north toward Colorado once again. For a few minutes we ride along in silence, but I can feel the weight of it. It doesn't just feel like we're driving to another place, it feels like we're driving toward the ending of a story.

"If you're having second thoughts, I can turn around," Scout says.

I notice her watching me out of the corner of her eye.

"You're not getting rid of me," I tell her.

"Is this because of what I told you last night?" Scout asks me. "Is that what made you want to come with me?"

I don't answer right away. I'm not really sure how to explain it.

"I'm out of reasons not to," I finally say. "Everything that ever mattered to me is gone."

"Me too," Scout says. Her eyes shift back to the road ahead once again and we drive for a while in silence.

I had always considered myself a good person before. Someone that tried to do the right thing. The only thought in my mind right now is revenge.

I know it won't fix anything. It won't bring Danielle back. It won't make a difference in the fate of the world.

But I don't care. I just want to kill as many of them as I can.

Revenge.

That feels like it's all I have left right now.

About half an hour after we cross the border we leave the highway and drive down the main street of a small town. Several corpses wander along the road. The walls of the buildings are covered in spray paint and pocked with bullet holes. So we drive on to another town.

We search for hours without luck. Just a few days ago they seemed to be everywhere. Now, the Reapers are nowhere to be found.

We stop for lunch and to set up the solar panel to charge the car. Scout sits on the front bumper beside me as we both take bites out of protein bars.

"Maybe we should go back to Cheyenne Mountain," I suggest.

Scout takes another bite from the bar and chews it while she considers this.

"Not yet," Scout says. "First we need to get some intel. Find out exactly what we're up against."

"Intel?" I ask. I'm not sure how she plans on getting that.

"We just have to be patient," Scout says. "Eventually, we'll run into one of their patrols."

We finish eating and pack up the charging kit when I hear the faint crackle of gunfire to the north.

"Did you hear that?" I ask Scout.

We both remain completely still and listen to the world.

A few seconds later, more rifles open fire in the distance.

"Let's get moving," Scout says and tosses the charger in the trunk.

We jump into the Tesla and Scout floors it. Her eyes are focused on the road as she speeds toward the sound of small arms fire.

I clutch my rifle tightly in my hands. There was a time when this would terrify me. Not anymore.

No matter how much I want to forget, I keep seeing Danielle in the clinic. The flesh ripped away from her face. Her emotionless eyes staring at me as she stumbled toward me.

Every time that memory pops into my mind, all I feel is endless anger and a desire to find those fuckers and kill every last one of them.

CHAPTER TWENTY-TWO

Scout pulls off the road near the edge of town and drives the car behind an abandoned factory to keep it out of sight.

Rifles still crackle nearby as we head toward the center of town on foot. Stitch trots along beside me, his nose sniffing the air. I can hear the men shouting and laughing in between the rifle reports.

We make our way along a residential street off the main strip, then we cut down an alley.

"Over there," Scout whispers and points to a delivery truck behind one of the stores.

I follow her over and she quietly climbs up on the truck. I bend down and scoop Stitch up in my arms and hand him to Scout before I climb on the truck as well. I take Stitch back from Scout while she climbs onto the roof, and then I hand him up to her before climbing up myself.

We crouch down as we scurry across the roof to get a look at the main road. When I peek over the parapet, I can see there are three vehicles. Two of them are their armored narco tanks and the other is a semi with a trailer.

They have a radio blaring heavy metal. As the dead emerge from the buildings and side streets, the Reapers gun them down. One guy wearing a clown mask is in the middle of the road with a machete. He hacks at a mangled corpse squirming in the road and cackles each time he swings the blade. Another man stands on a ladder and shakes a can of spray paint that rattles loudly. Then he tags the front of a building across the road. I duck my head back down instinctively when I spot him.

"I count ten so far," Scout whispers. "There might one or two more around here somewhere but nothing we can't handle."

I nod my head in agreement even though I really don't like those odds. Especially considering some of these guys are clearly psychopaths.

"You stay here," Scout says. "I'm going to circle around and take up a position across the street."

She pulls a pair of radios out of her bag and hands me one.

"Wait for me to give the word," Scout says.

"Got it," I say.

Scout moves back across the roof and climbs back down to the alley. I turn back around and watch the Reapers move around the street. I try to keep track of where they all are so I know where to aim when the shooting starts.

As the minutes go by, I start to get anxious. I peer over the edge of the building and look for any sign of Scout. It must be ten minutes since she left. I start to panic that something happened to her.

The radio finally hisses.

"Blake," Scout whispers.

I key the mic to respond.

"I'm here," I say.

"Get a target," Scout says.

I grab my rifle and lift the barrel over the ledge on the roof and take aim at one of the guys closest to the truck carrying a rifle.

"Blue shirt, near the truck," I tell her.

"I see him," Scout whispers. "Take him out."

As soon as I squeeze the trigger, I hear the rifle report across the street as well. My bullets tear into the abdomen of the man in the blue shirt and he crashes to the ground clutching at holes in his body.

I shift my rifle to another man with a submachine gun that is staring at the guy I just shot and squeeze the trigger again just as he turns his head to find out where the fire is coming from. The first rounds hit the dirt beside him, but one of them finds his face. He drops his gun as his hands come up to clutch at a hole in his cheek.

I shift the rifle again and point it at the man with the

machete in his hand. He looks around the street in confusion while he draws a revolver from his waistband.

"The roof," yells the Reaper with the spray paint.

The guy with the machete begins to raise the revolver but he is too late. My finger pulls back the trigger again and a trio of bullets hits him in the leg, the gut, and the last hits his shoulder causing the machete to fall to the pavement.

"Motherfucker!" he yells, but he manages to stay on his feet. The guy tries to level the revolver at me again, but I pull the trigger once more and he falls to the street.

I try to aim back at the Reaper with the spray paint, but I just see the ladder toppled over and a can of paint on the ground. The guy is sprinting for the truck. I center the rifle on the unarmed reaper and fire again. As soon as the bullets hit him, his legs give out and he crashes face-first in the street.

Before I locate another target, I hear something zipping through the air close to my head. I duck behind the parapet as more rounds hit the face of the building.

As soon as there is a break in the gunfire I sit up and aim the rifle, but when I get the man in my sights a corpse grabs onto him and tears into his shoulder. The man forgets all about me and pivots away from the zombie only to find there are several more of the dead beside him. He howls as they encircle him and drag him to the ground.

I consider shooting the man but instead watch as the

dead disembowel him with their hands while he screams and kicks in a puddle of his own blood.

It's over.

I look around the street one more time to make sure it's clear and then I stand up. The only sound is the stereo that is still blasting heavy metal and the dead moaning as they devour the man on the ground.

It was all over so fast. By the time they realized what was happening it was already too late. Killing them was so much easier than I thought it would be.

I swap a fresh magazine into the rifle and then pick Stitch up hop back down on to the roof of the truck in the alley. Stitch sniffs at the air and growls as soon as I set him down on the ground.While I make my way around the building, he follows right on my heels and turns his head from one side to the other to watch for threats.

As I approach the street, the corpses rise from the body on the ground and turn toward me. I stop walking and raise the rifle but I don't pull the trigger right away. I stare at the fresh blood dripping from their hands. The mangled faces are like horrifying masks, with human flesh dangling from their maws.

Stitch whimpers and lets out a panicked bark before he retreats behind me.

I know I need to pull the trigger before they get close enough to bite me, but I just can't do it. I can't take my eyes off the blood on their hands for some reason I don't yet understand.

Before I can piece it together in my mind, bullets tear through the skull of the female corpse in a long nightgown coming at me. She collapses in the street as more rounds take down the corpses behind her.

"Are you okay?" Scout asks me.

I lower the rifle and find her standing beside me. She stares at me through narrowed eyes.

"Yeah," I say.

"Why didn't you shoot them?" Scout asks.

"Gun jammed," I lie.

Scout shoulders her rifle and looks around the street once more to make sure it is still clear.

"Come on," she says. "I need a hand."

I follow her back up the block toward a man on the ground in the doorway of a diner. His hand clutches a gunshot wound in his knee. He grinds his teeth together and growls from the pain.

"Help me get him inside," Scout says.

She grabs one of his arms and I grab the other and we drag him across the ground and into the restaurant. He yelps in pain as we pick him up and set him down in a chair.

His long dark bangs hang over his face, like curtains around the dark circles of his eyes. He notices me watching him and he smirks.

"What are you looking at motherfucker?" he sneers. "Are you some kind of faggot or something?"

I get the urge to shoot him, but I just wait to see what

Scout is doing. She shrugs off her backpack and sets it on a nearby table.

Scout unzips the top of her bag. She digs around inside for a moment before she removes a long zip tie. After she closes her bag up again she steps behind the chair and grabs his wrists and secures them together.

"What now?" I ask her.

"I'm going to make him tell me what I want to know," Scout says.

CHAPTER TWENTY-THREE

"Who the fuck are you assholes?" the Reaper asks through clenched teeth. He tries to squirm in the chair and get his hands free from the restraint but gives up when he realizes they are too tight.

Scout ignores his question as she moves a table in front of the man. He watches as she picks up a rusty fork from a puddle on the floor and sets it down on the table. She pulls out her bowie knife and sidearm and places them on the table beside the fork.

The reality of what is about to happen here hits me. I stare at Scout trying to tell whether she is just trying to scare this guy or if she is really willing to follow through with all of this.

The man looks at the choices on the table. Then his

eyes study Scout for a long moment. His lips crack into a smile and he starts to laugh.

"You're not gonna do anything," the man laughs. "You're full of shit."

Scout sits down on the table and waits for the Reaper to stop laughing.

"They're gonna find you," he threatens us. "You have no idea who you're fucking with."

The man erupts into laughter again. He doesn't seem to notice as Scout picks the fork up off the table. She stands up and plunges the rusty fork into his gunshot wound.

The man tilts his head back and howls in pain at the ceiling as his body twitches and convulses from the intense pain. Scout twists the fork around. It might just be my imagination, but I swear I can hear the snapping of tendons through his screaming.

There was a time when something like this would have caused me to look away. Instead, I watch Scout closely. A wildfire burns in her eyes. There is no hint of any pity or remorse for the pain she is causing. She seems to enjoy watching this man suffer.

I feel a strange satisfaction watching it happen, too.

Finally, Scout removes the bloody prongs from the wound and the man stops screaming. His head flops forward. The intensity of the pain caused him to pass out.

Scout grabs a fistful of his long bangs and raises his head up. She slaps his face with her other hand a few times until his eyes open again. He winces from the pain as he comes to again.

"You crazy fucking bitch," he cries.

"Now that I got your attention," Scout says. "I want to ask you some questions. If you just tell me what I want, it'll persuade me to go easy on you. But if you don't, well... Let's just say I've been in your spot before so I know some ways to get what I want from you."

"I don't fucking know anything," he pleads.

"Is Andrew the one in charge of the Reapers?" Scout asks him.

"Who?" the man says.

Scout holds up the bloody fork again and points the tines at the wound.

"I swear," he says. "I don't know any Andrew."

"He was one of the men we picked up," Scout says. "Andrew and Shawn."

The man looks at Scout and then at me.

"Oh," he nods. "I get it. This makes sense now. You were with the people in the mountain. No wonder you are so pissed off."

"Andrew," Scout says again. "Is he the one in charge of the Reapers?"

"You mean Turner?" the man chuckles. "Nah. He isn't the boss. He is just, like, a captain. He was sent in after those bitches turned on us."

"What?" Scout says. "What are you talking about?"

The man looks at Scout and then at me.

"Oh shit," the man laughs. "You didn't know."

It starts to come together in my mind then, but I still don't want to face it. It can't be true.

"The women with those two little brats," he says. "They were supposed to put something in the water to make everyone sick. Then they would let us inside. They fucked up or something, though. So Turner decided to do it himself."

Scout turns to look at me for a moment as we both come to understand that he is talking about Amanda and Lacey. They working with the Reapers. The realization hits me like a knife to the gut.

"They were on your side?" Scout asks again.

"That's what we thought," the man said. "Until we found one of them with the kids inside. Then we knew. She swore she was still working for us, but... Turner decided not to take any chances."

Amanda was a part of everything that happened. All those people that died. She could have stopped it. Maybe Danielle might still be alive right now.

"The kids," Scout says. "Some of the kids are still alive?"

"I don't know if they are still alive," the man smirks. "But they were. They took at least five or six of them away."

"Where are they now?" Scout demands.

"I don't know," the man says.

Scout grabs his throat in her hand and squeezes as tight as can around his larynx.

"I don't fucking know where they took them," the man pleads.

Scout releases her grip on him and he coughs and winces in pain.

"I have no idea what they do with them," he finally manages to say. "They probably either put them to work or sell them."

"Who is in charge of the Reapers then?" Scout asks.

"I don't know his real name," the man says. "The sicarios only call him La Parca."

"La Parca?" Scout asks.

The man nods his head slightly.

"What the hell kind of name is that?" she asks him.

"It means the Grim Reaper," the man says. "Death."

Stitch lets out a growl behind me. I glance back and see a corpse approaching the building. One of the Reapers that we killed is back on his feet.

"I got it," I tell Scout.

She nods and returns her focus to the hostage in the chair.

"I want to know where they are right now?" I hear Scout ask him as I step through over the broken plates and debris sitting in puddles on the floor.

The man laughs.

"We are everywhere," he says. "You have no idea how much shit you're in. They will come looking for us."

Scout continues talking, but I stop listening as I focus on the corpse. I raise my rifle at his head as he steps on to the sidewalk. He moans and raises his arms as I step through the doorway and squeeze the trigger. His head snaps back and his knees buckle simultaneously and then the dead man falls forward. There is a crack as his skull hits the pavement.

I swivel to my left when I hear another moan. Another one of the Reapers has come back from the dead now and shambles toward me. I get the man in my sights, but then I hesitate and lower the rifle.

Behind him, I notice we have more undead coming our way. Maybe a dozen or more. It's nothing we can't handle, but getting out of here before we have to deal with them might still be the better option.

I raise the rifle again and fire a couple of rounds at the Reaper. The first shot goes right into his gaping mouth and the second punches through his forehead and then he collapses in the street.

When I turn around to head back inside, I notice more corpses are coming at us from the other direction as well. Stitch wags his tail anxiously and runs in a circle as he growls. I step through the doorway and clatter over the broken plates and cups.

"They all came up from Mexico when the outbreak started," the Reaper tells Scout.

"How many?" I hear Scout ask the Reaper.

"I don't know," he shakes his head.

"How many!" Scout demands.

"I don't know," he yells. "A lot. Hundreds. Maybe more."

"Hey," I interrupt Scout.

She turns around to look at me, her eyes still wild, pointing the knife in her hands in my direction. My eyes notice the fork inside the knee of the Reaper again and a gushing stab wound in his stomach.

"We're out of time," I tell Scout.

"I'm not finished," she says.

"We need to go now, Scout," I say.

Scout lowers the blade and puts it away as she gets to her feet. She grabs her sidearm off the table and slings her pack over her shoulder.

"Hey," the Reaper says. "Don't leave me here."

Scout glances back at him and then looks at me.

"Let's take one of the tanks," she says. "Might come in handy."

"Please," the Reaper begs. "I told you everything you wanted to know. You said you'd let me go."

Scout turns back around and faces the man in the chair again.

"No," she tells him. "I said I'd go easy on you."

She levels the gun at his face.

"This is me going easy on you."

"No, please—" the Reaper says before Scout pulls the trigger.

The bullet punches into his skull and then he slumps

forward in the chair.

"Let's go," Scout says coldly.

We leave the diner as the dead reach the intersection. Stitch starts to run back toward the road where we parked the Tesla until I call the idiot. He skids to a stop and turns and notices me heading for the narco tank, then starts sprinting back.

I lift up the hatch on the back of the vehicle and climb inside. The whole interior of the back is covered in foam insulation. All of the rear seats have been removed and a fifty caliber machine gun sits on top of a base bolted to the floor. I make my way to the front and sit behind the wheel.

"Let's go!" Scout yells as the rear hatch slams shut.

The hands of the dead start to pound on the thick steel plates of armor. The powerful engine roars to life when I turn the key. I sit up awkwardly in the seat in order to see the road through the narrow slit of bulletproof glass.

"Hang on," I yell before I shift the truck in drive and give it some gas. The armor wedge on the front of the vehicle makes short work of the dead. They crash into the steel and are flung aside.

I take a left turn and steer around the wrecked vehicles on the road. The narco tank bounces over the curb. Scout and Stitch tumble to the floor in the back as I swerve back toward the middle of the road.

"Sorry," I yell.

"Are you trying to kill us?" Scout yells.

"This thing is not exactly easy to drive!" I yell back.

We make it back to the derelict factory and I turn into the parking lot and drive to the back of the building. As soon as I come to a stop, Scout lifts up the back hatch. Stitch dashes out into the afternoon, relieved to be out of the tank.

"Think you can make it back in this thing?" she asks.

I check the gas tank that is down to about a third of a tank.

"I guess we'll find out," I tell her.

"Try not to kill yourself," she says as she lets go of the hatch. It crashes shut and then I wait while she hops in the Tesla with Stitch before I pull out in front of them and head back to the highway.

CHAPTER TWENTY-FOUR

Once we get back on the highway and the adrenalin rush subsides, I start to think about everything that just happened. It's a lot to process, but the empty vehicle and the open road leave me nothing to do but unpack everything that just happened.

All this time Amanda has been lying. I still can't believe she was there to infiltrate the base for the Reapers. I just can't believe that she could have changed so much that she would be capable of something like that. For all I know, maybe we still can't trust her.

It's her fault Danielle is dead.

The doctor and Claire.

The last hope that we had to survive this thing is gone because of her.

The thought makes me feel physically sick. I'm not sure

I will ever be able to look at Amanda again without thinking about what she has done.

I'm not sure I even know how to forgive something like that anymore.

This morning I had hope that killing the Reapers would make me feel better somehow. They had wronged us and it was the only way I could think of to make it right. But it still doesn't feel like we made anything right. Maybe we won't feel that way until every last one of them is dead.

I wasn't sure how I would feel after it was done. There was no guilt. I don't feel remorse or pity and anything at all.

But I am wondering if Scout is in control anymore. The only thing that scared me out there was Scout. I've never seen her like that. It was something I would not have believed she was capable of doing.

Maybe Scout is completely out of control. Maybe I am, too.

Not too long ago, I might have felt compelled to stop what happened today.

Now I just watched it happen.

And I felt nothing.

I feel like a line has been crossed and now that we've crossed it, we can't go back anymore.

This is the world we live in now and there isn't anything left worth saving. Not even us.

"Come in, Butch," a gravelly voice says.

I glance around and notice the CB radio attached to the

bottom of the dashboard. That must be how they communicate. My fingers feel around for the volume and I turn it up to listen in on the conversation.

"This is Butch," another man responds. "What you need, Skynet? Over."

"You reach Vail yet? Over."

"Not yet, Skynet," Butch says. "Still twenty miles out. Over."

"Copy that, Butch," the person going by Skynet says.

I lower the volume again. We didn't just get one of their tanks. Now we're tapped into their communications. We'll know exactly where to find them now. It will give us a major strategic advantage.

We're still just two people up against unbeatable odds. It's just a matter of time before they manage to kill us both. But I'm not going to make it easy for them.

They've destroyed any chance we had for turning this world around. The bastards have doomed us all. Amanda helped them do it.

The thought sticks in my mind the rest of the way home. I pull into the driveway at the ranch as the world turns away from the sun and the chill of night embraces the earth. I shut off the engine and climb out of the narco tank and head for the front door.

Scout watches me and I can only guess that she knows what is on my mind. She lets Stitch out of the Tesla and lingers outside as I go in the front door.

"Amanda!" I call out as I walk in the foyer. "Amanda!"

I run up the stairs two at a time and walk to the bedroom door. I twist the handle and open it up to find the empty room.

"Amanda!" I call out again.

I turn around and open the door across the hall, only to find that room empty, too.

Of course, she must have left as soon as she had a chance. I turn around in the hall and start back down the stairs. When I reach the foyer again, I fling open the door to tell Scout that she is gone.

"Blake?" Amanda says.

I turn around and look down the hall to see her standing in the kitchen.

"Is everything alright?" she asks.

"What were you doing?" I say as I walk toward her.

"I got scared here alone," she says. "So I went downstairs."

I reach out and grab her arms tightly.

"You lied to me, Amanda," I say. "You fucking lied to me."

"Blake," she flinches and takes a step back. "What are you talking about?"

"I know everything," I tell her. "They're all dead because of you."

"I don't know what you're talking about," she says.

I shove her backward and she crashes into a chair and tumbles to the floor.

"Stop! Blake!" Amanda pleads. "Let me explain. It's not

what you think. I didn't do anything, I swear. Once we got inside and I saw you were there, I told Lacey I wouldn't go through with it."

She breaks down into sobs and tears start streaming from her eyes. It seems real, but I'm not sure what to believe anymore.

"I was afraid to tell you," she admits. "I'm so sorry. You have to believe me."

"It was all an act," I say. "All that traumatized victim bullshit."

"No," Amanda says. "It wasn't. I wanted to tell you."

"Just stop talking," I warn her.

I turn my back to her and start to walk away. The idea of looking at her right now is just too much. I'm afraid of what I might do.

"You have to believe me," Amanda sobs. "I didn't want any of this to happen. Blake..."

I pause in the hallway but decide it's better to keep going before something happens that I can't take back. I walk out of the house again and find Scout standing on the porch in the moonlight. I let out a deep breath into the chilly air and watch it and listen to the crickets chirping in the dark.

"Sounds like that could have gone better," Scout says.

She rolls a small pebble between her fingers and then looks down at it and chucks it into the grass.

"This world is changing people," Scout says. "It's changing us, too. Not for good either."

I look over at her. The moonlight lights her face enough for me to see the scar below her eye.

"I don't think there is any way to stop it from happening," she says.

That's when I realize how this day has affected her, too. Stitch trots up on to the porch. His tail wags lazily as he sniffs around the boards and then sits down and stares at the moon.

"I can feel myself slipping away," Scout says. "And I feel like one day I'm gonna wake up and look in the mirror and not even recognize myself anymore."

"I think I know you mean," I say.

"I figured you did," Scout says. "You feel it."

"Yeah," I confess. "I don't think there is anything we can do about it."

A wolf lets out a long howl somewhere in the darkness nearby. Stitch cocks his head to the side and his ears perk up, but he remains in his spot on the deck.

"We can't trust Amanda," I say.

"You don't believe her?" Scout says.

I think about it for a few seconds and then shake my head.

"It doesn't matter if I believe her or not, though," I say. "We can't take that chance."

"I guess you're right," Scout says.

She lowers her eyes and stares at the grass for a few seconds.

"Lorento tried to warn me before," Scout says.

"About what?" I ask her.

"She told me if I kept taking people in that sooner or later I would end up getting all of us killed."

"No one could have seen all this coming," I say.

"I don't know," she says. "Maybe I would have if I wasn't too fucking stupid to listen to her."

"It isn't your fault."

Scout scoffs and folds her arms across her chest.

"Come on," she says. "Let's not turn this into some kind of bullshit pep talk. We both know I'm right."

"Scout," I say.

"I really don't want to hear it right now," she says.

"There's something else," I say. "There is a CB radio in the narco tank. That's how the Reapers communicate."

"That's good," Scout sighs.

"I heard them talking while I was driving," I say. "We'll know everywhere they are going to be."

She looks down at her hands again. I notice they are still caked in dry blood. She doesn't seem interested in the radio right now.

"Something wrong?" I ask her.

"It's been a long day," she says. She reaches down and snags the strap of her pack and hauls it up off the ground. "I'm gonna go change and turn in for the night."

She walks up the stairs and opens the front door.

"You coming in?" she asks me.

"In a minute," I tell her.

"Okay," she says. "Goodnight, Blake."

Then Scout shuts the door behind her and leaves me and Stitch on the porch.

I try to think about what lies ahead of us. I try to imagine how we get to some world that is better than this. But I can't see anything beyond tomorrow. I can't even imagine a world that makes sense anymore. The truth is I'm stuck here and there is only one way left to get out.

Stitch gets up and stretches his paws and stares at me. He ambles over to the door and sits there and waits for me to move.

I realize it's pointless to sit out here and drive myself crazy like this, so I turn and head inside. As much as I don't want to, I know I need to deal with Amanda again.

I go back inside and stand in the empty foyer. Scout left her pack on the bench beside the door. I unzip the front compartment and grab a pair of zip ties and close it up again. Then I march up the stairs and open the door to the bedroom where Amanda sits on her bed in the dark. She sniffs and wipes the tears from her eyes.

"Blake," she says.

"Shut up," I tell her. "Give me your arm."

She doesn't move so I reach down and grab it.

"What are you doing?" she asks. "Stop!"

I yank her wrist toward the bedpost and wrap the zip tie around them both while Amanda fights to free herself from my grip. Her arms are still thinner and weaker than they used to be.

"No, Blake," she begs. "Please don't do this."

"I can't trust you anymore," I tell her.

"Please, stop," she starts to cry again.

I grab her other wrist and this time she hardly fights as I zip tie her wrist to the other post. Once she is secure, I get up off the bed. I watch for a moment as she pulls feebly at the restraints.

"Blake, you can't leave me like this," she panics. "I can't go through this again. Let me go."

"It's your own fault," I tell her. Then I close the door and ignore the sobbing as I head to my bedroom down the hall.

CHAPTER TWENTY-FIVE

I wake up to the sound of birds singing outside the window. A cheerful sound that I can't handle for more than a couple minutes before it chases me out of bed.

I close the door and head downstairs. Scout is already awake and refilling empty magazines at the kitchen table. Her eyes glance up when I enter the kitchen, then she returns to her task.

She doesn't say anything as I walk by her and get a cup from the kitchen and pour myself some coffee. I suppose Scout heard Amanda crying last night. She stayed out of it, but I can sense she feels different about me this morning.

"I had to do it," I say.

Scout stops feeding bullets for a couple of seconds.

"I know," she says.

"It was just for the night," I say.

"You really think she'd try to hurt us."

I think about it for several seconds before I answer her.

"I honestly don't know anymore," I say.

"We can't leave her here alone then," she says.

"We'll have to take her with us," I say.

Scout twists around in her chair and looks at me.

"You sure that's a good idea?" Scout says.

"No," I say. "But we don't have much choice."

"I know this isn't the best time," Scout says. "But I feel like there is something you need to know."

Scout lifts the cup of coffee on the table and takes another slow sip before she continues.

"Before she died, Danielle told me something," Scout says. "She wanted to tell you, too, but she didn't know if you were ready to hear it."

She stops speaking for a few seconds and picks up the last empty magazine off the table. Then she puts it back down suddenly.

"Blake," she finally says. "Amanda is pregnant. Danielle knew it as soon as she came to Cheyenne Mountain."

"What?" I stammer. "Pregnant?"

I can hear the words that she is saying, but it comes as such a shock my mind can't make sense of any of it. I shake my head in anger and confusion. It's not just the shock of finding out, but that Danielle kept it from me, too. I can't understand it.

"Danielle had no idea how far along she was," Scout continues. She picks up the last magazine and begins to fill it again. "There was nothing in the lab, no ultrasound or anything. That's why she told me. She asked me to keep an eye out. She thought you would want to know for sure if it happened before or after all this."

"I don't believe this," I say. My legs feel unsteady so I walk back and lean against the kitchen island. I comb my fingers through my hair and scratch an itch on my scalp as I try to get my mind around it.

"I promised Danielle I wouldn't say anything," Scout says. "But I felt like I should tell you in case... I don't get the chance to later."

Scout stands up and grabs the full magazines off the kitchen table and shoves them into her pack. She slides her arms through the straps and pulls the backpack over her shoulders.

Scout pulls out her sidearm, ejects the mag to check it, and slaps it back.

"I'll be back in a little while," she says. I watch her as she walks down the hall to the front door.

"Where are you going?" I ask.

"We need to get some diesel for the tank," Scout says. "I'm going to check the other farm down the road."

"You shouldn't go alone," I say.

"I'll be fine," Scout says. She opens the door and then stops and looks back at me over her shoulder. "Be ready to go when I get back."

"We'll be ready," I tell her.

Scout closes the door and I take another sip of coffee

before I dump the rest of it in the sink and head back upstairs. I walk back to Amanda's room again and reach for the door handle, but catch myself before I open it. I let out a sigh and I tap my knuckle against the door several times.

There is no answer.

I open the bedroom door and find Amanda sleeping awkwardly in the bed. It kind of surprises me that she was able to sleep at all like that. I slip my knife from my pocket and open up the blade. Her eyes open up wide when I grab her wrist and she flinches when I cut the plastic tie.

She sits up in bed and rubs the red marks on her skin that outline where the straps had been.

"Thank you," she says.

"Don't thank me," I tell her.

I'm still angry about everything, but I realize I can't just leave her like that, especially in her condition. I start to leave the bedroom but before I'm out the door, Amanda calls my name. I still don't really want to talk to her, but I pause in the doorway and wait to hear what she has to say.

"Do you remember the morning this started?" she asks. "You called me."

It seems like a lifetime ago, but it is still something I'll remember until I die.

"I remember," I say.

"Right after that, someone shot me," Amanda says. She touches a hand to her abdomen. "Right here."

I turn halfway around and look back at Amanda sitting on the bed.

"I almost died," she says. "But there was a man that saved me. At least, I thought he was helping me. He kept me alive when I lost consciousness. Treated an infection. I thought I was lucky until I woke up one morning and I was tied up to the bed. It turned out he was a monster. He kept me like that for days. If it wasn't for Lacey I would never have gotten away from him."

I start to understand why she is telling me this now. It makes me regret what I did to her last night. My eyes look away from Amanda's face and stare at the plush carpeting on the floor.

"I didn't realize..." I say.

"I'm not about to let someone do that to me again," she says. She doesn't say it like a threat, but I can tell she means it. I may not trust her anymore, but I can still recognize she is being honest with me about this.

"I won't do it again," I say. "But I still don't trust you."

"Fair enough," she says. Her gaze falls to the floor and she nods her head.

"Get dressed," I tell her. "You're coming out with us."

Amanda looks up at me again.

"Where?" she asks.

"We're going after them," I say. "The Reapers."

"What?" Amanda says. "No. You can't. It's crazy!"

"Get dressed," I tell her again.

"Blake," she says. "You have to listen to me. You have no idea what you're up against."

I ignore her and walk back down the hall. In the

bedroom, I grab a clean pair of jeans that belonged to the previous owner and try them on. They are a little loose in the waist, but I cinch a belt around them. They will have to do. When I look up, I notice Amanda standing in the doorway.

"I already figured out who we are up against yesterday," I tell her. "You don't need to remind me."

The comment causes her to stop in her tracks for a moment.

"Blake," Amanda says. "This isn't about me. The Reapers are psychopaths. You're going to get killed."

I take off my shirt and toss it on the floor.

"Then I guess we'll finish what you started," I say.

She stares at me in shock while I turn away and pull open a drawer on the dresser and dig through the shirts there to find something that will fit.

"What does that mean?" Amanda says.

I grab a black long sleeve shirt from the drawer and slam it shut.

"Everyone is dead because of you," I say and jab a finger at her chest. "If you would have been honest from the start we would have been able to stop it. All those people would still be alive right now."

Her eyes fill with tears again and I can tell she is about to cry, which only makes me even more pissed off at her for some reason. I pull the shirt over my head and shove my arms through the sleeves.

"Get dressed and meet me downstairs," I tell her and

then I push her aside and make my way to the door. "Unless you want me to tie you up again."

Fifteen minutes later, Scout returns and we all get into the tank. Amanda climbs into the passenger seat and I crouch beside Stitch just behind the front seats.

"They're sending another team down now," Scout informs me.

"Where?" I ask.

"A few miles west of the town we were in yesterday," she says. "They were sent down to look for the other team. We can probably be there waiting for them."

"Let's get moving," I agree.

Scout shifts the narco tank into drive and we rumble over the dirt driveway toward the road. We ride along in silence and listen to the conversations on the CB radio.

"This is a big mistake," Amanda finally says. "You have no idea what you're getting us into."

She sure has a lot to say all of the sudden.

"These people won't stop until we're all dead," she adds.

Scout looks up at the rearview mirror and makes eye contact with me.

"I wish you would have felt the need to warn us like this back in Cheyenne Mountain," I say. "A lot more people would be alive if you did."

That comment shuts her right up.

She clenches her right hand into a fist and presses it to

her lips while she stares out the passenger window in silence.

We drive back through the town where we fought the Reapers yesterday. Then we head to the next small town a few miles up the road. This town is really only a few small buildings just off the highway.

Scout drives near a gas station and brings the narco tank to a stop in the middle of the road. She peers through the bulletproof glass at the other nearby buildings.

"We should have maybe thirty minutes before they come through here," Scout says.

"How do you want to play this?" I ask her.

"You stay here in the truck," Scout says. "I'll get into position at the gas station to flank them."

"I don't really like being the bait," I tell her.

"You'll be fine in here," she says. "It will look like the truck is abandoned. They will have to get out of their vehicles to check if anyone is inside here. Once they are in the open, let them have it."

It certainly sounds simple enough. I nod to Scout and then she squeezes by me and climbs out the hatch in the back of the vehicle. Through the filthy front window, I watch as Scout jogs across the road to take up her position at the gas station. Scout climbs on a dumpster and then climbs up on to the roof. She squats down and props her rifle between the letters of the sign.

Amanda stares at me. Even though I'm not looking at her right now, I can feel her eyes watching me. I try to ignore the sensation and keep an eye on the road and wait for the Reapers to appear.

"Blake," Amanda says.

"Not now," I say.

"You're not like this," Amanda says.

"Like what?" I say.

"Like them," Amanda says and gestures with her hand toward the road where I watch for approaching vehicles. "At least you didn't use to be."

"A lot has changed since then," I say to her.

"That's not what I mean," she says. "You're smarter than this. The man I knew would never bet it all when the odds say you have no chance to win."

Her words register, but I stop paying attention when several dark shapes appear on the horizon.

"They're coming," I say.

I reach for the rifle and check to make sure the safety is off and the mag is full while Amanda starts nagging me again.

"Later Amanda," I tell her.

"Blake," she pleads. "It's not too late. We can just drive away before they get here.

"Shut the fuck up," I snap.

My aggressiveness gets her to finally shut up, but I start to wonder if she is trying to argue with me to tip them off to our presence. Amanda shrinks away from me when I yell at her, but I notice how close she is to the front seat. She could easily reach over and lay on the horn to give us up. I don't know for sure that I can't trust her, but I can't take any chances either.

"Get over here and be quiet," I whisper to her and gesture toward the wall behind me in the rear cabin with the muzzle of the rifle.

Amanda nods her head and then relocates herself behind me. I check the window again to see how close the vehicles are getting and try to keep an eye on Amanda moving around in the periphery. It's not really possible to monitor her movements while facing the window.

I turn around and stare at her for a long moment. If I get too distracted when the shooting starts, she could try to run out the hatch and escape or go for one of the other guns around us.

Even though she is not the same anymore, I still don't think she would shoot me in the back. But I have to admit it's a possibility. I guess I'll just have to take my chances.

The three vehicles slow down as they approach the truck. The first vehicle looks like it was probably a sports car that has been fitted with a turret and a machine gun. Another vehicle was once an ambulance that is now covered in thick steel plates. There is also a massive vehicle, maybe a dump truck, with an armored canopy built over the open bed in the back.

My mouth feels dry and I lick my lips and close it and watch nervously as the vehicles pull to a stop in the road. For a minute or two, the convoy just idles in the street. Maybe they suspect something is up.

The radio beneath the dash comes to life.

"Skynet, this is Bones. Come in," a woman transmits.

Hearing a woman in their ranks surprises me. It seems out of place. All the Reapers I'd seen so far were men.

"This is Skynet. Go ahead," another voice responds.

"Located one of the vehicles," Bones says. "Looks abandoned. No sign of survivors."

Then there is a short pause before Bones continues.

"Strange," she says. "There doesn't appear to have been much of a struggle either. We're checking it out now. Over."

"Copy that," Skynet responds. "Over and out."

A few seconds later, several men emerge from the vehicles followed by a woman carrying a large backpack and a medical bag. I'm going to take a wild guess that she is the one that goes by Bones. While the four of them approach, three more men exit the trucks. Their squinting eyes scan the surrounding area.

I raise the rifle to my shoulder and prepare to open fire on them.

"Ready, Blake?" Scout whispers over the radio.

I grab the radio hanging from my belt.

"I'm good," I whisper. I move closer to the murder hole but keep the tip of the tip of the muzzle inside the truck.

"Fire," Scout says.

A gunshot cracks the silence. The man closest to the gas station on the right side of the road is the first to go down.

The back half of his head explodes into a red mist and then he flops on the pavement.

The other three stop walking and glance back at the man that just fell. Then their rifles come up and they crouch in the road. Another round from Scout drops a big guy with a mohawk right before I open fire with the assault rifle. My first shots drop the last guy beside Bones. The woman yells something and gestures wildly at the gas station, then lays down on the pavement and crawls for the closest abandoned car.

I have a clear shot at her, but I notice the other Reapers that were guarding the trucks running up the road. One of the men fires wildly at the gas station. The other two men point their rifles at the truck and I see the muzzle flashes and hear the loud thunk of the bullets hitting the thick armor of the truck.

"Shit!"

I flinch away from the sudden impact of the rounds against the metal. Even though the bullets can't get through the armor, I still feel like one of them might find the murder hole a hit me. When I try to look out at the street again, I can't locate a target. I sweep the street several times.

The crack of a rifle shot from Scout shatters the air. A long string of shots from an assault rifle answers back in response.

The Reapers must all have found cover. It's hard to tell what is happening when I'm looking through a tiny hole in the side of the van. More rounds spray the side of the van and I retreat from the opening again. When I look out to the street again, I finally get a visual on one of them. A guy with a bandana on his head peers at the truck over the trunk of a car.

"Got you," I say and squeeze the trigger.

He drops back into cover as the bullets strike the rear window. That's when I hear the radio squawk.

"Blake!" Scout yells. "They're right on you!"

My heart starts pounding as I turn to look at the street again. I don't see any of them. I can't understand what she means.

Suddenly, the hatch on the rear of the truck flies open and light floods into the dimly light cabin. My first thought is that Amanda must have seen how distracted I was and is trying to take off. As I turn to look, I see the dark outline of a man pointing a gun at me.

Before I can get the assault rifle free from the murder hole, I hear the shot. A moment later I feel the stabbing pain in my midsection. My hand reaches for the area as I collapse against the wall of the van.

The man adjusts his aim and then my eyes stare down the dark black hole of the barrel.

"No," I stammer.

I close my eyes as he pulls the trigger.

Amanda screams.

A gun fires and then there is a second shot a second later.

Somehow I'm still alive.

I open my eyes to see the man staggering back into the sunlight. He stares at the reddening hole in his shirt.

Several more shots knock the man down for good.

I look beside me at Amanda. Her shaking hand still holds the pistol that she had used to shoot the man. I turn and notice the bullet hole in the foam insulation right beside my head. Amanda must have fired just before he pulled the trigger.

She saved my life.

Then the pain in my chest reminds me that I might still be dying, though.

"Fuck," I mumble as a clutch at the wound again.

Amanda turns at the sound of my voice and drops the gun. She crawls over to me and sobs and softly touches my face and holds my hand.

"I'm okay," I assure her, even though I don't know that for sure.

The radio squawks again.

"Blake!" Scout yells.

I force myself to sit up even though the pain is excruciating. My hand reaches the radio and I push the talk button.

"I'm here," I say. "I got hit. I think I'm okay."

"Thank god," Scout says. "They're all down except for the chick. She is pinned down behind that white sedan. I think she is out of ammunition. Can you move?"

"I think so," I tell Scout.

"Good," Scout says. "I want her alive."

"Got it," I groan.

I grab my rifle and fight through the pain to get to my feet. The world starts to spin as I try to step out of the back of the van. My eyes go blurry and then I feel myself falling and everything goes black.

CHAPTER TWENTY-SIX

The next thing I hear is music. Peaceful music accompanied by a woman singing softly.

I open my eyes and find that I am back at the ranch in bed with a scruffy dog lying next to my foot.

Then the singing starts again. I look over and see a woman with black hair sitting in a chair in the corner of the room. She stops singing when she notices me looking at her. It takes a moment before I recognize her.

"You're—" I say. My throat is dry and my voice, raspy. I can't remember her name. Panic sets in as I try to recall what happened. For just a moment, I'm afraid I'm being held captive.

Then I notice she is not just sitting there, the woman is tied to the chair. I notice my hands are free. When I make a move to sit up a sharp pain in my shoulder hits me and I lay back down on the bed and reach my hand up to find the bandage there.

The rest of what happened begins to come back to me. I was shot.

"You should try not to move too much," the woman says. "It will just open your stitches."

The dog lifts his head up and stares at the woman suddenly.

"Your name is Bones?" I ask.

"Bones." She smiles. "It's just something they called me. Not my name."

"You a doctor?" I ask her.

"I guess," she says. "I used to do autopsies. Now, you could say I'm a doctor. As much of one as you're going to find anyway."

She smiles and it seems sincere enough, but it doesn't matter. It's not like I can trust her. The world is not like that anymore. I turn my eyes away from her and stare up at the ceiling.

"It's kind of surprising," I say. "You don't seem..."

I hesitate when I can't find the words.

"What?" Bones asks.

"Like the kind of person that would..." I trail off again.

"Hang around a bunch of criminals?" she says.

"Yeah," I nod.

"It's not exactly like that was my first choice," Bones scoffs.

I turn my head to look at her again and her eyes look

away toward the light coming in the window and she shakes her head. I can tell she feels like I won't understand what she is thinking. Maybe I won't.

"You've seen what they do," I say.

Her front teeth dig into her lower lip then she lets out a defeated sigh.

"Yeah," she says. "I've seen it."

I wait for her to say something else to justify her decision but she remains silent.

"They killed hundreds of people in Cheyenne Mountain. Innocent people. Kids. Scientists that were trying to stop this. They even killed the president."

She turns her head back to look at me and her eyes meet mine.

"Scout already told me," she says. "There was nothing I could have done to stop what happened."

A disgusting taste fills my mouth. Even though I know what she says is true, it makes me sick that someone could stand by and watch it happen and do nothing.

"I can tell you think I'm a monster just like the rest of them," she says. "But I've never hurt anyone. I'm just trying to save people. Anyone I can save. Including myself."

My lip curls into a smirk and I shake my head.

"You think you're better?" she snaps. "I watched you kill people. And I still saved your life after you did it."

"What the hell is going on up here?"

Scout steps into the doorway and glares at Bones and then her eyes settle on me.

"You feel okay?" Scout says.

"I've been better," I say.

"You're lucky to be alive," Scout says. "According to her anyway."

She jerks her head to the side to indicate Bones.

"I sure don't feel lucky," I say. "Lucky would have been not getting shot in the first place."

Mentioning getting shot reminds me of exactly what happened. How I would have died if Amanda had not saved me.

"How is Amanda?" I ask Scout.

"She's fine," Scout says. "She's finally asleep. She wouldn't leave the room before."

"She saved my life," I tell Scout.

"Amanda told me everything that happened," Scout says. "Well, after I thought she was the one that shot you and nearly killed her."

"How long was I unconscious?" I ask.

"Couple days," Scout says. "More from the concussion than the gunshot."

"Concussion?" I say as I reach a hand up to my head. I feel a thick bandage wrapped around my skull.

"You hit your head pretty hard when you collapsed in the street," Bones interjects. "I gave you some stitches there too."

Stitch lifts his head up and again and looks around, confused.

"At gunpoint," Scout clarifies.

"I would have done it anyway," Bones says.

"I'm sure," Scout scoffs.

A long silence hangs in the air. Scout walks across the room and stands behind the chair and stares down at Bones. Then she reaches down and cuts the ties around her wrists.

"So what happens to me now?" Bones asks.

Scout just gives her a hard look.

"I did what you wanted," Bones says. "I treated him. I told you, I am not going to hurt any of you."

"I know you won't," Scout says. The way she says it I can tell she does not mean that she believes Bones, but that Scout knows she would never give her the chance.

"Please," Bones says. "Tell me what I have to do to prove myself."

"Get up," Scout says.

"I'll tell you anything you want to know," Bones says.

"We'll see about that," Scout says. "Walk."

Scout shoves the woman in the back and follows her out into the hall. As she closes the door, Scout pauses and turns back.

"I'll be back in a bit to check on you and bring you some food," Scout says.

"Thanks," I say.

Scout starts to close the door again.

"Scout," I say. "Don't—"

I start to say not to kill Bones but, I look at the softening expression on her face and realize that I don't have to.

"Don't worry," Scout says softly. Then she closes the door quietly and leaves me and Stitch in the room alone.

I manage to scoot my body until I am sitting upright in bed and then I gently peel away the bandage and inspect the hole in my upper chest. There is still a huge bruise all around it. It hit me right above the top of my lung and below my shoulder.

I wonder if there is an exit wound on my back. I try to move my left arm slightly, but the pain is too intense. When I take a deep breath my entire upper body aches as well.

The only thing I know for right now is that I won't be going out anytime soon. It was probably a mistake in the first place. Something like this was bound to happen.

I probably should be dead. I'm just not sure whether I feel lucky to be alive or not yet.

Scout and I went out there to fight because we had nothing to lose. We knew the risks, but that didn't stop us. The fact is, I think that deep down we both felt that we just want this to all be over and the only way that will happen is by dying. Death was what we anticipated.

But things don't always turn out the way you expect.

My mind keeps replaying my memory of being shot over and over. I remember feeling surprised and then relieved. It's kind of depraved, but I even felt a strange sense of satisfaction that Amanda was there and that she would have to see how much I was suffering.

Then I remember her holding the gun right after she killed someone to save my life. I remember how Amanda looked as I stared up at her in the moments after. She didn't fire that gun because she was afraid for her own life. Amanda just did not want to lose me.

Maybe we can't go back to our lives before, but that doesn't mean we aren't still the same person deep down. Broken and scarred, but still the same.

I want to believe that, but I'm not sure that I do.

Maybe it's at least worth sticking around to find out.

Scout returns a few minutes later. She carries a plate with a sandwich (peanut butter and jelly), an apple from the tree outside (sliced), and a few chocolate chip cookies. It's like she made this lunch for a toddler.

"Thanks," I say.

"Sorry," she says. "I didn't feel like cooking."

"It's fine," I tell her. "I appreciate it."

I pick up the sandwich even though I'm not sure my stomach can handle it after going a couple of days without food. Still, it would be a shame to waste the bread. I can't believe they have a loaf that is still fresh.

"What did you do with her?" I ask Scout.

I sink my teeth into the bread. It's dry and chewy. Freezer burnt.

Disappointing.

"Locked her in the pantry," Scout says. "Had to switch

out the doorknob with one from the bedrooms that locks. She could probably get out if she tried but she hasn't yet."

"You can't keep her in there forever," I say.

"I know," Scout says. She sits down in the chair that Bones had been tied to a short while ago. "I was going to kill her as soon as I knew you were going to be okay."

"But you're not going to," I say.

"No," Scout shakes her head. "She might still be useful to us."

"Useful how?" I ask.

"She might be willing to help us locate Stevie," Scout says. "And then there is Amanda."

I know she means the baby.

"She said she would help us," Scout says. "Not sure if I believe her just yet, but I guess it's enough reason to keep her alive for now."

She might not be ready to admit it yet, but I get the sense that Scout has already decided against killing our prisoner. I understand why Scout changed her mind. As much as I want to direct all my anger and rage over what happened at Bones, I can't either. She is just a person caught up in this like the rest of us.

Besides, what happened with Amanda and Bones made me realize that giving people another chance might just save my life one day.

CHAPTER TWENTY-SEVEN

As darkness descends outside, someone knocks softly on the door. Since waking up, I managed to get up and even washed up a little, before the pain drove me back into bed. I've been laying here for a few hours and am not exactly sure if I was just sleeping or not.

"Yeah," I say.

The door opens a crack and Amanda puts her head through the doorway. I can barely see her face with the lights off.

"Can I come in for a minute?" she asks.

"Please," I say. "Can you get the lights?"

She flips a switch next to the door and a lamp in the corner turns on. The sudden change requires me to squint against the blinding light to make out much of anything for several moments.

"I can come back later if—"

"It's fine," I interrupt her. "I was waiting for you to wake up so I could talk to you."

"Oh," Amanda says. Her surprise is apparent in her voice. She steps into the room and closes the door quietly behind her.

"Please," I hold out a hand toward the chair near the bed and wait while Amanda sits. She clasps her hands together in her lap like she used to whenever she was about to have a serious conversation.

"I wanted to thank you for saving my life," I tell her. "I know I haven't exactly been very understanding about everything. It's just been kind of hard to makes sense of all of it."

After I finish speaking, her eyes watch me for what seems like an eternity.

"So," I continue. "I guess I'm trying to say, I'm sorry for—"

"Blake," she interrupts me. "It's okay. You don't need to apologize for anything."

"No," I say. "I do."

"I wasn't honest with you," Amanda says. "I wanted to tell you from the beginning, but I was too scared."

"If it wasn't for you I'd be dead right now," I say. "I should have been more understanding after everything you went through."

Amanda swipes away the moisture around her eyes.

"Everything is just so fucked up now," she laments. "I

hate it. It shouldn't be so hard to do the right thing, but half the time I don't even know what that is anymore."

"Me either," I say.

Amanda gets up from the chair and comes closer to the bed. She kneels beside the bed and drapes an arm across my uninjured shoulder and rests her head there.

"I'm glad I didn't lose you again," Amanda says. "I'm not sure I'd have been able to handle that."

I move my hand and put it on her arm and hold her there for a long moment. It still feels strange and unfamiliar, but I feel like it might not be that way forever anymore.

Stitch lifts his head up off the bed and his ears perk up. Then he gets to his feet and lets out a growl.

Amanda picks up her head and looks at the dog.

"What's with him?" she asks.

"He hears something," I say. "Quiet, Stitch!"

Once he shuts up again so I can listen, I hear it too. It sounds like vehicles coming toward us from the highway. A lot of vehicles.

Stitch starts barking loudly.

"Get the lights," I tell Amanda.

She gets up from the bed and hurries across the room and flicks the switch to leave us in darkness. I manage to sit up in spite of the crushing pain in my upper body with every breath I take. Through the window I see the headlights coming down the road in the darkness. There are at least a dozen vehicles, maybe more, heading straight for us.

"It's them," Amanda says. "They found us."

The door bursts open and Scout appears in the doorway. She has a rifle in each hand and one slung over her shoulder. I wonder how she could have gotten them so fast. Maybe she had been anticipating this.

"We got company," Scout tells us.

"I see them," I say while I grab a shirt slung over the bedside table and go about the awkward process of putting it on.

The Reaper convoy is stopped on the highway at the edge of the property.

"Think they know we're here?" I ask Scout.

Scout walks over to the bed and sets a rifle down on the bed beside me. She stares out at the road.

"Seems that way. One of their scout patrols rolled through here a few hours ago. I already hid the narco tank in the barn, but they might have noticed the fresh tire tracks or something."

"Looks like a lot of them," I say.

"I know what kind of shape you're in," Scout says. "But I'm going to need you."

"I'm good to go," I assure her.

Scout nods and turns to Amanda.

"You too," she says.

"Me?" Amanda says.

Scout hands Amanda the other assault rifle. Amanda takes it and shifts it in her hands. She still holds it awkwardly. It's pretty clear she has relied on others to keep her alive before now.

"You know how to shoot one of these?" Scout asks.

"I think so," Amanda says.

Scout glances at me. I detect grim hopelessness in her eyes. Our chances of getting out of this alive are pretty bad. We all know it.

Light moves across the room as the vehicles begin to move again and turn down the driveway.

"Here they come," Scout says.

"What's the plan?" I ask Scout.

"We'll hold them off as long as we can," Scout says as she hands me a couple of full mags from her pack. "If they get in the house we can fall back to the bunker."

"Got it," I say.

She turns to leave and I watch her walk into the hallway. I get that ominous tightening in my gut as she disappears down the stairs. It feels like that might be the last time I will see her alive. Maybe none of us will be alive in a few minutes.

I take up a position at one window and Amanda crawls to the other side of the bedroom and peeks out at the narco tanks pulling up outside the house. Stitch starts barking again and runs downstairs when I tell him to shut up. His barking trails off as he moves downstairs and then he growls at the front door. Probably thinks he can scare them all off. Stupid dog.

I watch for several tense minutes as the vehicles idle out front. They turn on a couple of spotlights and shine them on the house, but no one gets out of the vehicles.

"What are they doing?" I ask Amanda.

"How the hell should I know?" she says.

Stitch starts barking again downstairs as the lights shine through the windows.

Then muzzle flashes blink from the side of the truck and bullets tear through the exterior of the house. I duck down as one of them strikes the window just above my head. A moment later the shooting stops. I lift my head up again and stare at the window.

The glass is still intact. Bulletproof.

The people that owned this place really thought of everything.

Several men emerge from the truck carrying guns.

I reach up and unlock the window and crack it open just enough to fit the barrel through. I hear shots from the lower level. One of the men falls to the ground and clutches his leg in agony. The rest of the Reapers open fire again.

More bullets tear through the house. The windows may be resistant, but even smaller caliber bullets tear through the walls. I hear a thunk as a bullet strikes the house near me and realize there must be some kind of armor panel below the windows as well.

I notice Amanda trying to crawl toward me.

"Don't move!" I yell and then it feels like a vice tightens around my lungs. I'm not sure if she can hear me over the gunfire, but she retreats back to the window and covers her head with her arms.

After a few more seconds without dying in the hail of bullets, I sit up and start firing back at the figures I can make out in the darkness. One guy makes a run for the door, but Scout takes him out before he even gets to the porch. I manage to hit a couple of Reapers that were firing from behind the narco tanks when they stay exposed for too long.

The guns stop firing again after a couple of minutes. A haze of gunsmoke hangs in the air. I swap in a fresh mag. The spotlight shining through the bulletholes covers the walls around us with yellow spots.

I spot some figures getting out of the trucks. They race into the tall grass to try and flank us. I put my eye to the scope. The night vision makes it easy to track them. I open fire and take out two of them. Scout takes out the third.

There must be close to a dozen dead bodies scattered in the yard already, but I would guess we are still vastly outnumbered. There is no way we can hold them off forever, but if we can hold out and take out a few more of them, maybe they will decide it isn't worth it.

No one moves outside for the next several minutes.

"What are they doing?" I ask Amanda.

"I don't know!" she repeats.

Eventually, a few more figures emerge from the darkness. In their hands, they hold some bottles with burning rags sticking out the top.

Molotov cocktails.

The Reapers heave half a dozen bottles into the night

sky. The containers shatter as they strike the exterior of the house. The liquid erupts into a ball of fire and bathes everything in an orange glow.

I scurry across the room to Amanda and yell for her to move as the Reapers open fire outside again. Amanda crouches down near the floor and runs into the hall as bullets punch through the walls all around us. We get downstairs and I look around for Scout but I don't see her anywhere.

"Go," I push Amanda down the hallway as more rounds dent the steel front door. The entire front of the house is already engulfed in flames. The fire climbs the walls and stretches across the ceiling. I can hear the wooden beams crackling. Maybe all of the bullet holes in the house are giving the fire more oxygen. It seems to be spreading so fast.

We reach the kitchen and then, through the smoke, I see Scout by the pantry.

"Come on!" Scout yells. "You'll die if you stay here!"

Bones coughs as she ducks beneath the layer of smoke and hustles toward us. I usher her toward the stairs that lead down to the bunker and then turn to see Scout coughing and fighting to breathe through the smoke.

"Scout!" I yell.

She drops to the floor and coughs and gasps for air. I turn around and go back to help her. I grab hold of her clothes and drag her across the tile. The smoke burns my eyes. Tears streak down my face and I can barely see.

Then I hear Stitch barking. He must have already run downstairs. I follow the sound and drag Scout to the stairs. Amanda and Bones both come out of the bunker to help me get Scout to safety. Finally, I slam the steel door of the bunker shut and seal us all inside.

CHAPTER TWENTY-EIGHT

Inside the bunker, we listen to the dwindling gunfire and the burning house crashing down above us.

All of us are collapsed on the floor gasping for air, except for Scout. I look over to where she is motionless beside the door. Scout is not breathing.

"Help her," I urge Bones.

She takes another breath, looks at me, and then Scout. Bones crawls a few feet over to get to Scout and checks her vitals before she starts performing CPR. Even though everything hurts right now, I force myself to sit up and watch as Bones compresses Scout's chest and counts.

After thirty seconds or so, Bones stops the procedure. I can't tell if she is giving up or if she is just still struggling to breathe herself.

"Keep going," I urge her by gesturing with the rifle in my hand.

She leans down and opens Scout's mouth and fills her lungs with air again and resumes compressions. Finally, Scout coughs and sucks in a deep breath of air and then coughs again.

"You're okay," Bones says and rolls Scout to her side. Then she looks at me and nods before she collapses against the shelf of canned food behind her and wipes the sweat from her brow with her forearm.

A booming crash above us rattles the shelves inside the bunker. The frame of the house must be starting to collapse. A split second later the halogen bulbs overhead blink out and immerse us in total blackness. A red emergency light mounted on the wall of the bunker goes on a moment later.

I stay by the door with the rifle ready. I don't hear gunshots above us anymore. The Reapers must have thought we were consumed by the blaze and took off.

The fire roars on above us. The support beams of the house that had been our last refuge crumble and crash down. My entire body aches. I look down and notice the spots of blood on my shirt. The stitches must have opened up again.

"Let me have a look at those stitches," Bones says.

The scruffy dog thinks he hears his name. He trots over from the sleeping area of the bunker and licks her face. She politely nudges him out of her way, but he just wags his tail and tries to lick her face again until she shoves him back. Then he breathes loudly through his nose and sits down beside me and watches while the woman looks at my injury.

"It looks like you need some stitching," she says. "I don't have my stuff though."

"I remember seeing some first aid supplies down here somewhere," I tell her.

She nods and checks on Scout again before she gets up to search through the supplies on the shelves.

Scout coughs a few times and then finally manages to push her body off the floor and sit up. Another part of the house crashes down and she looks up to the ceiling for a moment and I can see the dark soot covering her face. She lowers her face and cups her hand over her eyes.

"My head is throbbing," Scout says.

"You inhaled too much carbon monoxide," Bones says. She grabs some noisy packages off the shelf.

"At least we're still alive," I say.

"Thank God for that," Scout scoffs and then looks at the floor again.

I realize she still feels like she doesn't have anything left to live for. That was how I felt just a couple of days ago. But sitting here now, I realize that I actually meant it. I am glad to still be alive.

We might be buried alive. Everything around us is crumbling. Our chances of surviving much longer are pretty bleak.

In spite of all that, I still feel lucky to be alive.

Amanda appears out of the darkness and settles down beside me. The dark bloodstain on my shirt draws her eyes.

"I'm okay," I say.

I put my hand on top of hers to reassure her. More thunderous noise as the house caves in further. I have to wonder what could possibly be left up there. My eyes look around the dim light of the bunker. It might have saved us from the fire and the Reapers, but it could just be a giant coffin.

"We're going to be buried alive down here," Scout says.

For a second, I wonder if I had been talking out loud. It's like she can hear my thoughts.

"I thought you said it would be safe?" Amanda asks. Her eyes dart between me and Scout.

"We're alright for now," I say.

"Until the backup power runs out," Scout coughs. "Then we will run out of air."

"How long until that happens?"

"A couple of days," I say. "Maybe more. If we're lucky it will give us time to dig ourselves out.

Bones returns with some medical supplies, water bottles, and a tank with a mask. She sets the tank down and checks the hose to make sure it is connected to the mask.

"I found this along with some hazmat suits back there," Bones says. "Not really how they were meant to be used, but it will work. Put it on."

She holds the mask out for Scout, but Scout just holds up a hand to say no.

"I'm fine," Scout coughs.

"Just put it on," Bones says.

Scout reluctantly takes the mask and pulls the strap over her head. Bones twists the knob on the tank and it hisses softly as it pushes oxygen through the tube.

"Good?" Bones asks.

Scout takes a deep breath and blinks her eyes and gives Bones a thumbs up.

Then Bones turns her attention to me. She unbuttons the top of my shirt and pushes it aside to remove the old bandage that is soaked through with blood. She takes out a bottle of something and cleans the open wound again.

I watch her face while she works on me. She seems too focused on threading the needle through my skin to notice me. Finally, she finishes up and applies a new bandage to the wound.

"Try not to move around too much," she says.

"Thanks," I say.

"Yeah," Bones mumbles. She starts to grab up the packing and bloody gauze on the floor.

"I'm sorry we dragged you into the middle of this," I say.

"I was already in the middle of it," she says. "Don't worry about it."

"If we get out of here alive," I say. "You can leave."

I look at Scout. I can't see her expression behind the gas mask, but she gives a slight nod of agreement.

Bones smiles for a second, then she lowers her eyes.

"I'll have to think about that," she says. "The truth is I am glad to be away from them. At first, I thought all of you were monsters too. Just like them. But you're not the same."

Bones stares at something right in front of her face that only she can see.

"The things they do to people," she says. "I told myself that it wasn't my fault because there was nothing I could do. I just stood by and watched it all happening and did nothing."

"Watched what?" I ask her.

"They have hundreds of people," she says. "Innocent people. Survivors. Locked up in cages. Anyone that refuses to join them. They sell some of them. The women. The children. The things they do to them…"

I look over at Scout again and I can see the expression of horror on her face.

"They're sick," Bones says. "You people had a right to want revenge. I used to have kids. If I thought they had my child I would have reacted the same way as you."

She gets to her feet and looks at me and then at Scout.

"If we make it out of here," Bones says. "I want to get as far away from here as possible. But first, I will help you look for that little boy."

Then she takes away the wrappers and discarded bandages to throw them in the trash.

The fire burns into the night. Once I no longer hear the sounds of the house collapsing, I check the steel door to find it is still hot to the touch. I imagine on the other side the burning embers and ash smother the entrance.

On the wall, the clock reads midnight. I close my eyes and manage to sleep for awhile sitting upright with my rifle. I haven't heard any sounds to indicate the Reapers have stuck around, but there is no point in taking any chances.

When I wake up, I find everyone else is asleep. I check the bunker door to find it's still warm, but not as hot as it was. It's been about 8 hours. The fire should have completely burned itself out at this point.

I decide to open it up. As soon as the door is opened blackened wood and ash and debris spill on the floor. Smoke and soot fill the air and I cough and cover my face with my arm in a futile attempt to shield my eyes. The rubble shifts in the stairwell and then slits of sunlight peak through.

When I turn to look behind me, I find everyone is awake and watching me.

"It looks like we'll be able to get out of here," I inform them.

"Hello?" A man's voice calls out above me.

I spin around suddenly and raise the rifle in my hands.

My first thought is that it must be one of the Reapers. They waited around to find out if any of us survived.

"Is anyone alive down there?" The man has a Hispanic accent.

There is a long pause.

"I thought I heard someone," the man says again.

"We saw this place burning from miles away," says a woman. "Look around. There is no way anyone could have survived this."

"Hello!" I call out.

"What are you doing?" Scout hisses. She grabs her rifle off the floor and gets up. I hold up a hand to stop her.

"It's okay," I tell her.

I know I'm taking a risk, but these people aren't with the Reapers. They said they weren't here yesterday. They just saw the fire. I could be wrong but my gut tells me that I should take a chance on these people. We need all the help we can get right now.

There is a long silence in response to me. Maybe they didn't hear me. Perhaps, I was wrong. Maybe I should not have taken a chance on trusting them.

Of course, it could just be that they aren't sure if they should trust me either. I think I might hear some voices whispering above, but I can't be sure.

"Where are you?" the man finally calls back.

"Down here!" I yell as much as I can with my hoarse voice. The ash is already in my throat.

"I can't see you," the man says.

A figure above blocks the sun momentarily.

"Right here," I say. "The fire buried us. Can you help dig us out?"

The debris above us shifts. Then there is another long pause and I hear them whispering but can't make out the words.

"How many of you are down there?" the man says.

I look at Scout and she shakes her head in disapproval of everything.

"Four of us," I tell him. "And a dog."

"A dog?" another man says. His voice is different. I hear a slight southern accent when he says the word dog.

I start to wonder how many of them might be up there, but I'm not sure if asking that is a good idea or if I'd get an honest answer anyway.

"Please," I cough. "We need help. We have some food and supplies. We can share some with you if you get us out."

There is another long pause.

"Yeah, homie" the first man says at last. "Hang on. We'll help get you out."

Amanda and Bones help to remove the remains of the house from the bottom of the stairs, while Scout stays ready with the rifle at the door in case things go bad.

"I'll be right back," I tell them.

With my injury, I can't help much to move the debris, so I pack up some stuff from the bunker. We can't stay here, but there is still a lot of food, supplies, and ammo that we'll need. I don't mind sharing with the people that are helping us, but I'm making sure we have everything we need first.

I locate a few backpacks and start packing clothes, refilling empty magazines, and packing food and water as well as I can using one arm. When I try to move my other arm the pain gets too intense. I can move my elbow, but if I shift my shoulder in the slightest the pain is unbearable.

By the time I'm done with the supplies, they've nearly managed to clear the stairwell. I stand by Scout with my rifle ready in case things go south.

"Don't even think about trying anything," the man with the southern accent warns. "I got a bigass army out here."

His muffled threat gives me a reason to doubt my decision for a moment. I glance at Scout and she tightens her grip around the rifle. The fact is it doesn't seem like there are more than one or two people clearing the debris up there. It has to be a bluff. I shake my head to let her know I don't think we'll really have to fight.

Finally, the scorched remains of a wall are lifted up and sunlight floods the destroyed staircase. A stocky Hispanic man with arms that are thicker than my thighs looms in the opening for a moment. His eyes quickly take stock of us and our weapons.

"It's okay," he assures us. "No need for the guns, amigos. Come on."

We all slowly climb out and emerge into the morning

sunlight. I try to look around to see how outnumbered we are but my eyes still have to adjust to the light.

"Holy shit," says a familiar voice.

I lift a hand to my brow to shield the light and blink my eyes. Then I see a familiar face beneath the brim of a cowboy. It's a face that I never thought I'd lay eyes on again.

CHAPTER TWENTY-NINE

"Fletcher?" Scout says.

"Get over here," Fletcher says.

Scout runs over to him and wraps her arms around him. She lays her head against his chest and holds him for a long moment before she pulls away and looks at his face again. She unwraps her arms from his waist but places a hand on his chest.

"Oh my god," Scout gasps. The shock of seeing him again has her short of breath. "You're alive?"

I'm pretty stunned, too. I just stare at him with my jaw hanging open. It's like seeing a ghost.

"Of course, I'm alive," Fletcher says. "I'm too pretty to die."

He looks at me, then at the other faces of the people with us that he doesn't recognize. I can tell he is concerned that there aren't more of us. Stitch jumps up against his leg and whimpers for attention.

"Easy boy," Fletcher reaches down and pats his head. The scruffy little mutt licks at his fingers until Fletcher retracts his hand and wipes it dry.

"I can't believe it," Scout smiles. It's the first time she has smiled in what seems like a long time.

"So," Fletcher says. "You're it?"

I take that to be his way of asking if we're the only ones that survived.

"Yeah," I manage to say. "Chase and Natalie, too. But they took off."

Fletcher nods solemnly. He takes a moment while that settles in. I am sure he isn't completely surprised to find out how many people didn't make it, but it doesn't make it any easier to swallow.

"I'm sorry. I—" his voice trails off. I haven't really seen Fletcher at a loss for words before, but I understand it now. "I'm glad as hell to see you guys."

"Who's this?" he asks and gestures as Amanda and Bones.

"This is my wife," I tell him. "Amanda."

His eyes open wide for a moment.

"You're shitting me," he says. Then he dips his hat toward Amanda and touches his finger to the brim. "Pardon my language."

"It's okay," Amanda smiles.

"This is Bones," I say.

She still seems a little unsure about all of us but offers up a smile.

"What the hell kind of name is that for a good looking gal like you?" he asks her.

"Hey," Scout shoves him weakly in the chest.

"I'm just saying," Fletcher deflects.

"I have you back two minutes and already—" Scout says.

"Now, come on," Fletcher says. "I didn't say it like that."

I had realized the two of them were getting kind of close before, but apparently they were more involved than I realized. I glance over at Amanda. She watches the two of them with a smile. When her eyes turn to me, I get uncomfortable and look away. The moment just feels awkward.

I clear my throat.

"Bones was just a nickname," I say. "She was with the Reapers, but she is okay."

The big man that I first saw when we climbed out of the bunker shoots a look at the woman beside him and then they both stare at Bones.

"Reapers," Fletcher says.

"You know about them?" Scout asks.

"Yeah," he says. "We know who they are."

He takes his hat off his head and combs his fingers through his overgrown hair and looks around at the smoldering ruins around us.

"So that's what happened here," he says. "La Parca."

"We should get going, homie," the big man says.

"Chill out, bud," Fletcher says. "We're fine. Besides, can't you see we're having a moment here?"

Fletcher notices me eyeing his two companions.

"Thought you had an army?" I ask him.

"Shoot," he says and snaps his fingers. "I'm being rude. That's Elise and Armando. Just call him Army."

"I don't like that," says Army. "That's not my name. Mando or Arm—"

"It sounds way fucking cooler," Fletcher says. Then he looks at me for agreement. "Am I right?"

"You shouldn't listen to him," Army says. "Stupid fucking *puto*."

"Don't mess with me and my Army," Fletcher says raising up his fists and throwing soft playful punches at Armando. The big man swats his hand away.

"The dead are headed this way," Army says and raises a finger toward a ridge along the northern horizon. "We can't be fucking around here all day, homie."

"Those motherfuckers got to be five miles away," Fletcher says. "Go smoke some more bud and relax or something."

The big man turns and wanders off a few feet.

"He's okay," Fletcher says quietly. "He helped me out of a jam back at that hotel. Saved my ass a bunch of times, really."

"I still can't believe you found us," Scout says.

"It wasn't that hard," Fletcher smirks. "I just followed

the damn smoke. Could see that shit for miles. I should have known I'd find you two at the source of it."

I am still in shock. Not just because Fletcher is alive. Something about him always made me think he'd survive this whole thing. It's also that he is still the same. Nothing seems to affect him much. I haven't been around someone like that in a while. He's a little much to handle right now.

"I wanted to go back a look for you," Scout blurts. "I tried."

"Hey," Fletcher hugs her again. "It's okay."

"They told me you were dead," Scout says.

"Don't beat yourself up," Fletcher whispers. "There was nothing you could have done to help me out of there anyway."

"I'm so glad you're here," Scout says. "Everything has been so bad since we lost you."

"I knew this was going to happen," Fletcher says. He glances at me for a moment. "I told you Lorento was just going to get us all killed."

"We made it to Cheyenne Mountain," I tell him. "It was still there."

"Was," Fletcher says.

"There were hundreds of people," I said. "The president, well acting president, too. It wasn't for nothing."

"What happened?" Fletcher asks.

I look at Amanda for a moment and then at Scout. It's not really going to do much good to bring it all up again. I try to think of the simplest explanation possible instead.

"La Parca," I say.

"Son of a bitch," Fletcher mumbles.

"They killed Danielle," Scout sniffs. "They killed the doctor and Claire. They killed everyone."

"Stevie?" Fletcher asks.

"I don't know," Scout says. "I don't know what happened to him."

"Goddamn," Fletcher shakes his head and stares down at the ground for a long moment. "This just ain't fucking right. We went through too goddamn much to have it all be for nothing."

He fights off the emotions that are about to overcome him and swipes away at his eye.

"Damn ashes," he says. Even though it isn't that ashes.

Scout reaches up and wraps her arms around him again.

"I'm alright," he insists but hugs her back.

Then I look at him and Scout and I look at Amanda. This was not the ending that any of us had hoped for. We like to imagine we're the heroes here to save the world. It seems like we were dead wrong.

Unless this isn't the end at all. Maybe we still are the heroes.

"Things don't always work out the way they're supposed to," I say. "That's just reality. But wasn't all for nothing."

"Fletcher!" Army says. "We just going to wait for those fucking *muertos* to come eat us or what, homie?"

"Damn it, Army!" Fletcher yells. "I told you, I'm having a goddamn moment here. Go start the Jeep or something."

Fletcher shakes his head. His mouth cracks into a smirk and just like that he is back to himself. It reminds me of when I first met him back in Chicago. Through all of this, he is still the same cocky bastard that he's always been.

"We don't have much room in the jeep," Fletcher says. "What else you guys have down there?"

"A few more guns," Scout says. "Couple thousand rounds of ammo. Food."

Fletcher whistles.

"I'm tempted to take all that and leave your asses here instead."

Scout scowls at him and he gives her a wink.

"Just kidding," he grins. "We'll come back for it tomorrow."

He jerks his head toward the Jeep in the driveway where Army is already behind the wheel and Elise sits in the passenger seat. We all crowd in and hang on to the roll bars as we rumble over the bumpy gravel toward the highway.

CHAPTER THIRTY

The Jeep takes us back across the border into Colorado as a thunderstorm rolls in along the western horizon. Lightning flickers in the distance and the rumbles of thunder growl a little louder with each passing mile.

"Little Bear," Fletcher yells to be heard over the air rushing all around us. He points dead ahead of us to a snow-capped mountain surrounded at the base by towering evergreens. "That's home."

Army drives through a pair of tiny towns, both are just a handful of shops and restaurants and a couple of blocks of houses. Everything has been destroyed by the Reapers. He takes a left down a small side street that goes on and on in a straight line through the wild brush.

We turn off on to a ghost of a road that looks like it was once dirt. The wild grasses have already reclaimed the land.

We cross a field at the southern face of the mountain and into the woods. Army slowly steers between the trees and then pulls to a stop beside a rusty old pickup. I look around, however I see nothing but woods in every direction.

"There's nothing here," I say.

"No shit," Fletcher says. "Come on, we got to get moving unless you want to be out here when that storm rolls through."

I ease down from the back of the Jeep and look up at the mountain. Stitch hops down after me and trots off to the nearest tree and sniffs it and then decides against peeing on it and moves on to another tree.

"How far do we have to walk?" I ask.

"Just up there a ways," Fletcher says pointing vaguely toward the western slope of the mountain.

"It's about five miles," Armando says.

"Five miles?" I say. With my shoulder, I'm not so sure I can hike five miles up a mountain.

"Army what the hell you have to say that for?" Fletcher says.

"It's five miles," Army shrugs.

"He isn't going to want to do it now," Fletcher says.

"I'm just not sure I can do it," I say.

"See?" Fletcher shakes his head at Army. He walks over and grabs the strap of my backpack from my hand and tosses it at Army. "You get to carry his stuff now."

We set off over the rocky ground and make our way

around the southern face of the mountain as the looming storm drifts closer and closer.

"We're out in the middle of nowhere," I say.

"That's the whole idea," Fletcher says. "Tim lives—"

"Tim? Your brother?" Scout says. "He's alive?"

"Of course he's alive," Fletcher says. "He's my brother."

Fletcher talks as though it's inconceivable that anyone closely related to him could ever possibly die. Although considering that seems to be the case with Fletcher, maybe there is something to it.

"Anyway, I told you before he always had a place way up in the mountains," Fletcher says. "No one is crazy enough to come looking up here. Not even the fucking stiffs. Oh hell—"

Fletcher stops abruptly.

"What is it?" Scout says.

"I just stepped in some bear shit," he says and wipes his boot against the dirt.

Elise lets out a quiet laugh. Fletcher glances over his shoulder at her.

"You mean scat," Elise says. It's the first time I've heard her talk.

"No, I'm pretty sure it's shit," Fletcher says.

Elise starts laughing even harder.

"I forgot to mention Elise is Tim's girlfriend's baby sister," Fletcher says. "She's also annoying as hell."

"Thanks, old man," Elise says. She doesn't look that

young. Maybe her mid-twenties, but Fletcher seems to see her as a younger sister.

Being around Fletcher makes me feel better, but I try not to laugh because it is just too painful. I start to struggle as we climb higher up the mountain. Maybe it's the altitude. It makes me breathe heavier which makes the aches in my chest even more excruciating.

"How much farther is it?" I finally have to ask.

"Not far," Fletcher says, which I assume to be a lie. "You still whine just as much as I remember, Blake."

"I got shot," I remind him.

"Yadda, yadda. Did he always whine this much, Amanda?" Fletcher asks.

Amanda looks up at him for a moment. She seems surprised to have a question directed at her.

"Umm," Amanda says softly. "I guess he always was this bad."

Fletcher laughs loudly. Amanda glances back at me and I can see a hint of a smile at the corners of her mouth.

"I thought so," Fletcher says.

We eventually reach a clearing with a shimmering lake. The face mountain and the grey clouds reflect off the surface.

"Little Bear Lake," Fletcher says. "We catch some cutthroat trout there. That's our main food source."

"You will get so sick of eating fish," Army says. "Every day more fish."

"There's home," Fletcher says.

He points ahead to a log cabin across the lake. A trickle of smoke drifts out of a pipe on the roof. A few solar panels are mounted on poles in the yard.

"Tim built this place all by himself," Fletcher says.

"Because he is way more useful than you are," Elise says.

Fletcher looks back at her again.

"What did I ever do to you?" he says. Then he holds a hand up before she can speak. "No. Don't answer that."

A chilly breeze drifts over the mountain and makes me wish I had something more than a flannel shirt on at the moment. It reminds me that winter will be here soon and finding enough food to survive won't be getting any easier. But at least we won't have to worry about the dead coming way up here.

As we approach the house, thunder crashes loudly and then the first drop of cold rain starts to fall. We pick up the pace but the downpour hits before we get around the lake.

Stitch spots the cabin and takes off. The dog barks and yelps at the door. It's like the rain is killing him. The front door opens and a man pokes his head outside and then Stitch runs right into the house. The man just watches him go by him and then spot us approaching and leaves the door open even though he heads back inside. By the time we rush through the front door, we're already soaking wet.

A tall guy in his early thirties with a beard stands next to a woman with long blonde hair by the wood-burning stove in the front room. In her arms, she holds an infant who stares at us with curious blue eyes. That must be Fletcher's brother and his girlfriend. And they have a child.

Tim isn't just tall. With the tight thermal shirt he's got on, it's pretty easy to tell that he all muscle, too. Not to mention his girlfriend looks like some kind of fitness instructor herself. Hard to believe she could have just had a kid so recently. Must be the mountain life.

"Just made it back in time," Fletcher says. "Well, almost."

Tim smiles at Fletcher, but he doesn't look all that happy to see us crowded together in his house.

"Who are these people?" Tim asks him.

"These are my friends," Fletcher says. "The ones I told you about. Well, some of them."

He turns and puts an arm behind Scout's back.

"This is Scout," he says.

Tim's expression brightens instantly and he reaches out to shake Scout's hand.

"Scout," Tim smiles. "So good you're here."

"Fletcher wouldn't shut up about you," his girlfriend smiles.

"You mean he wouldn't shut up," Elise mutters.

Fletcher ignores her insult and looks at me instead.

"That's Blake," he says wagging a finger at me. "And his wife, Amanda. This young lady goes by Bones."

Tim gives us all a nod of acknowledgment. His girl-friend holds up her hand and waves.

"That's my little brother, Tim, and his girlfriend, Stacy,"

Fletcher says. He walks over by Stacy and takes the tiny hand of the baby and wiggles it so as to make the kid wave at us. "And this handsome little guy is C.J."

Stitch runs into open space in between all of us and shakes his body, spraying all of us. Then he wags his tail and starts sniffing at the shoes of the new people.

"Damn dog," Fletcher says.

Tim laughs and reaches down to pet the dog on the head.

"That smelly beast is Stitch," Fletcher says. "He's smarter than he lets on."

"Come on in guys," Tim says to us. "Get warm. I'll grab you some dry clothes."

"I'm just finishing dinner," says Stacy. "I'm sure you all must be hungry."

"I'm always hungry," says Army. "Just look at me."

"I'll give you a hand, Sis," Elise says. She strips off her jacket and hangs it by the door before following Stacy into the kitchen.

A chill causes me to shiver and goosebumps to erupt all over my arms, so I crouch close to the fire to try and catch as much heat as possible.

"You okay?" Bones asks me.

"Just a little cold," I say through chattering teeth.

She squints her eyes slightly and then reaches out and puts the back of her hand against my forehead and holds it there for a moment.

"I'm alright," I assure her.

She pulls her hand away and doesn't say anything but I can tell she is concerned I might have symptoms of some kind of infection.

The decor inside of the cabin is pretty sparse. There are a couple of old couches. Some family pictures on the wall. An American flag. Near the kitchen is a small wooden dining table and chairs that appear to be handmade. The whole place is dim and smells of smoke from years of burning wood.

Lightning crackles outside followed by a long rumble of thunder that causes the ground beneath my feet to tremble. The sound makes Stitch all anxious and he presses his body against my leg and pants heavily.

I pat him on the head to help him relax. He closes his mouth and sniffs at the air for a few seconds and then follows the smell of cooking meat into the kitchen.

Tim returns with some dry clothes for each of us and hands them out.

"Thanks," I say when he hands me a pair of sweatpants and a shirt.

"Those are mine," he says. "So they might be a little too big."

"Did you build this place by yourself?" I ask him.

"No," he laughs. "Not by myself. Stacy and Elise helped. Unfortunately, we don't have a whole lot of space, but we'll figure out a way to make it work."

"This place is great," Scout says. "Thank you."

"Hey," Tim smiles. "No need to say thanks. My brother

was going crazy without you. I'm glad he found you. Now we all get some peace and quiet hopefully."

I head down the hall to get changed in the bathroom. I strip off my wet, dirty clothes. Then I put on the sweatpants and the hoodie that are a couple sizes too large. It's not a great look, but at least getting into the warm clothes makes me feel better right away.

When I head back to the kitchen, Stacy hands me a hot bowl filled with some kind of steaming meat and beans and vegetables.

"This will warm you up," she smiles as she offers me a spoon.

I thank her and then try to find a spot somewhere in the crowded house.

"Here," Tim says. He gets up from his chair. "You can sit here."

"No," I say. "I'm fine. Really."

"No you're not," he says. "Sit down. I insist."

I relent and put my bowl down and collapse into the seat.

"Are you sure you're related to him?" I ask Tim. I point my spoon at Fletcher in the chair across the table from me. "You are so much more polite than he is."

It's about as much as I can contribute to the conversation.

"I got the good looks and he got the manners," Fletcher says.

"I'm pretty sure he got both, Chuck," Army says.

Tim leans back against the wall and watches and chuckles to himself.

"Nobody asked you, Army," Fletcher says. "Fucking traitor."

I take a bite of the meat in the dish and even though I have no idea what kind of animal I'm eating it still tastes pretty good. The entire bowl is devoured within a couple of minutes. I immediately start to get so tired that my eyes just continue to close on their own. I can't even remember how long it's been since I slept.

As soon as Scout, Amanda and Bones finish eating we all say goodnight. There are only two beds in the whole house, so I take one of the couches and fall asleep within seconds of closing my eyes.

CHAPTER THIRTY-ONE

I wake up early the next morning. When I sit up on the couch, I find Army snoring on the floor beside me. Through the window, the shapes of the trees outside can barely be seen in the darkness. Across the room, I see Elise on the other couch in the dim light. Bones is asleep on the floor beside her.

After I get up as quietly as I can and go to the bathroom, I find Stitch waiting for me in the hallway. He stretches his legs and yawns and then walks over by the front door.

"Alright, stupid" I whisper to the dog. "I'm coming."

We step out into the grey twilight of the approaching dawn. Drops of water fall from the tree branches and land on the damp forest floor.

I follow Stitch toward the lake that is shrouded in a

layer of fog. While he gets to work sniffing the base of every tree, I sit down on the huge stump of a fallen pine near the water and listen to the birds. Soon the sun starts to rise over the mountains to the west. It's about the most peaceful morning I've ever experienced, even before all this.

Still, I'd be lying to myself if I didn't feel an unresolved tension.

I know I should be glad that we found this refuge up in the mountains, but deep down I can still feel this incredible void.

When this all started, the only thing I wanted was to get to my family. Now I have. All that is left of my family anyway. It's just hard to accept because it's nothing at all like I envisioned it.

The world we used to know is gone. The people we knew are gone. Even the ones that are still alive. None of us are who we were.

A stick snaps behind me and I look back to see Amanda approaching from the house. She makes her way down to the lake.

"Good morning," she says.

"It is," I agree. "Better than most."

"It's so pretty up here," she says.

I watch her staring over the lake. The shadow of a cloud overhead drifts across the face of the mountain on the other side of the water.

"Is it okay if I sit?" she asks.

"Of course," I tell her.

I scoot over a few more inches to make room and she settles down on the other half of the large tree stump.

"Is everything okay?" she asks.

Instead of answering right away, I think about it for a long moment.

"No," I say. "It isn't. I guess it seems like that's how it should be after everything we've been through."

Amanda presses her lips together and stares down at the earth.

"We have been through a lot," she says. "Both of us."

I don't say anything, but I think about everything that happened up until now.

"Do you think we will ever be okay?" she asks.

"No," I say. "I don't think we will be."

Amanda tilts her head back and stares up at the clouds moving across the sky and thinks that over.

"Is it mine?" I ask her.

She turns her head back toward me again and creases appear on her brow as she searches my face.

"How long have you known?" she asks me.

"Not long," I say.

She looks away from me and sighs.

"It's not yours," she admits. "I'm sorry. I was trying to find a way to tell you."

"It's okay," I say.

The door of the house opens and closes again, and I look back to see Fletcher in front of the house. He shakes his head and mutters to himself.

"Scout wants to go back and look for that little boy," she says.

"Stevie," I say.

"Fletcher tried talking her out of it," she says. "But she won't let it go."

"I know," I say. "She won't."

Amanda looks at my face for a long moment then she lets out a long sigh.

"You're going to go with her," she says.

It isn't a question, because she already knows what I'm going to say.

"Damn it, Blake," she says. "Just let it go."

"I can't," I tell her.

"It's over," she says.

"No," I turn to look at her. "It's not over. It never will be."

Amanda lowers her eyes to avoid my gaze and clenches her teeth.

"I don't want to lose you," she says. "Not again."

I feel bad for not being able to lie to her and pretend everything will be okay. So I put an arm around her and pull her close. She rests her head against my good shoulder and is happy to just stay there with me for a while.

The truth is, I'm still not sure who we are anymore. I just know neither of us is the same person we used to be.

Maybe there will come a time when I look at her and I won't think of the daughter we lost. Seeing her won't make me think of Cheyenne Mountain and the Reapers. I may not think about what happened to Danielle.

But I'm not there yet and I don't know if I ever will be.

I remove my hand from around her back and stand up.

"I'm going to get ready," I say.

She nods her head. I linger for a long moment and then turn to look at the vast mountain range along the horizon.

I get the urge to say something more to her, but I can't find the words. They just aren't inside of me. I'll have to keep looking for them out there.

"Come on," I call Stitch. "It's time to go."

EPILOGUE

This is not how I ever pictured that the end would happen. From the very beginning, I believed that somehow things would be okay.

I was wrong.

Things will never be okay.

Flakes of snow slowly drift down on us as we hike along the rocky mountainside.

"Hold up," Tim says when we reach a bluff that overlooks the valley below us. "We'll rest here for five minutes."

I shrug off my pack and drop it on the powdery white layer of snow on the ground.

"I'm too fat for this shit, homie," Army says to Fletcher. He hunches over with his hands on his knees and tries to catch his breath.

"Builds character," Fletcher says and pats the big guy on his shoulder.

"*Pinche culero,*" Army mutters.

"I don't know what the hell that means, but I'm going to take it as a compliment," Fletchers smiles.

Scout unzips her pack beside me and pulls out a pair of binoculars. She raises them to her eyes and scans the countryside.

"Looks like you were right," Scout says to Bones.

"Of course I was," Bones says.

Scout hands the binoculars to me.

"It looks like they still have people locked up there," Scout says.

I take a look for myself at the prison in the valley below. From this distance, I can't make out much, but I do see a number of people huddled around fires in the prison yard. Guards in the watchtowers watch over them.

According to Bones, these are people that the Reapers are holding against their will. I can't be sure she is telling the truth about that, but it sure does look that way.

"Can you tell how many tangos are down there?" Fletcher asks me.

I try to count the people with guns that I can see, but there are too many.

"No," I tell him.

"Take a guess," he says.

"A lot," I tell him.

"I thought you were supposed to be a numbers guy," Fletcher shakes his head.

"You really think we can do this?" Elise says.

Fletcher looks at Tim. It turns out that Fletcher's little brother is not only much bigger than him, but he is also a Green Beret. The man has been part of Army special forces operations all over the globe. Taking on the Reapers doesn't intimidate him at all. Tim has faced people like them time and time again. He is the real deal.

Tim gives Fletcher a nod.

"We got this," Fletcher assures her.

"I sure hope you're right," Elise says. "I don't feel like dying today."

"I'd never let that happen," Tim says.

"Because you love your future little sis," Elise smiles.

"Because Stacy would kill me when I got home," Tim corrects her.

Fletcher bumps fists with his brother and the two have a laugh.

"Shut up, Chuck," Elise says.

"You guys ready?" Tim asks.

"No," Army says. "I'm not ready."

I look over to find him collapsed in the snow.

"Damn it, Army," Fletcher says.

"Just go ahead without me," he says.

"Get off your ass," Fletcher says. He walks over and holds out a hand and helps the big guy to his feet.

"Let's get moving," Tim says. "We got people to save."

There were a lot of choices I made that turned out to be wrong. Some of them cost people their lives. This may turn out to be one of them, too. There is just no way to know until it happens.

Looking back I would have done so many things differently. But even if I had done them differently I don't know that it would have mattered.

We pick up our gear again and follow Tim through the mountains. I stare at my feet as they march through the snow and I think about Amanda back at the house. She did not want me to come out here. After everything that happened to her, she has had enough. She just wishes I would let it go, too.

But I can't do that. None of us can. Not after everything that they destroyed.

It can't all be for nothing.

That is what it will be if we just give up. If we were to accept this as the ending.

That's not something we're willing to accept.

We'll keep fighting until we make a world that is worth living in again or until there are none of us left.

So, this is not the end.

ACKNOWLEDGMENTS

Continuing my series this far would not have been possible with the help of my biggest supporters— my wife Sarah, and my two daughters Camille and Eliza. I owe a special thanks to countless other friends and family that have helped me along the way and continue to support me on my writing journey. Of course, these stories would not have happened without the best fans that continue to come back for more. Thank you all for the support!

ABOUT THE AUTHOR

Jeremy Dyson lives for one reason... To kill zombies. Until he gets that chance, he occupies his time drinking beer and writing stories.

After accumulating debt at the University of Iowa, Jeremy moved back home to Illinois, worked on a farm, built websites, made lattes, wrote how-to articles, and took dogs for walks before deciding he should consider doing something different with his life.

He currently resides in the cozy town of Crystal Lake, Illinois with his wife, two daughters, their dog, and his best friend Jason Voorhees.

Okay, I just made that last part up.

If you have enjoyed this book, please take a moment to leave a review to show your support of the author.

Thank you for reading.

BOOKS BY JEREMY DYSON

REALM OF THE DEAD SERIES

Rise Of The Dead

Return Of The Dead

Rage Of The Dead

Refuge Of The Dead

and coming soon...

Remains Of The Dead

Made in United States
Orlando, FL
21 December 2021

12323275R00189